SEAL'S RESCUE

Bone Frog Brotherhood Book 4

SHARON HAMILTON

SHARON HAMILTON'S BOOK LIST

SEAL BROTHERHOOD BOOKS

SEAL BROTHERHOOD SERIES
Accidental SEAL Book 1

Fallen SEAL Legacy Book 2

SEAL Under Covers Book 3

SEAL The Deal Book 4

Cruisin' For A SEAL Book 5

SEAL My Destiny Book 6

SEAL of My Heart Book 7

Fredo's Dream Book 8

SEAL My Love Book 9

SEAL Encounter Prequel to Book 1

SEAL Endeavor Prequel to Book 2

Ultimate SEAL Collection Vol. 1 Books 1-4 /2 Prequels

Ultimate SEAL Collection Vol. 2 Books 5-7

SEAL BROTHERHOOD LEGACY SERIES
Watery Grave Book 1

Honor The Fallen Book 2

Grave Injustice Book 3

BAD BOYS OF SEAL TEAM 3 SERIES
SEAL's Promise Book 1

SEAL My Home Book 2

SEAL's Code Book 3

Big Bad Boys Bundle Books 1-3

Christmas Bite Book 3

Midnight Bite Book 4

THE GUARDIANS

Heavenly Lover Book 1

Underworld Lover Book 2

Underworld Queen Book 3

Redemption Book 4

FALL FROM GRACE SERIES

Gideon: Heavenly Fall

NOVELLAS

SEAL Of Time Trident Legacy

All of Sharon's books are available on Audible, narrated by the talented J.D. Hart.

ABOUT THE BOOK

Navy SEAL Tucker Hudson has barely recovered from his last difficult deployment in Africa, a near-failed operation, when he learns the American hostage they were unable to free that last time, has been found. His team is tasked with going in a second time to complete what was left undone.

Brandy Hudson's world is changing every day as she devotes herself to their new pregnancy and the purchase of their new home.

But danger from the hostage rescue across the oceans comes home to affect Brandy and Tucker's family in a desperate plot uncovered in California. Will it be in time to save the happily ever after they both desire?

AUTHOR'S NOTE

I always dedicate my SEAL Brotherhood books to the brave men and women who defend our shores and keep us safe. Without their sacrifice, and that of their families—because a warrior's fight always includes his or her family—I wouldn't have the freedom and opportunity to make a living writing these stories. They sometimes pay the ultimate price so we can debate, argue, go have coffee with friends, raise our children and see them have children of their own.

One of my favorite tributes to warriors resides on many memorials, including one I saw honoring the fallen of WWII on an island in the Pacific:

"When you go home
Tell them of us, and say
For your tomorrow,
We gave our today."

These are my stories created out of my own imagination. Anything that is inaccurately portrayed is either my mistake, or done intentionally to disguise something I might have overheard over a beer or in the corner of one of the hangouts along the Coronado Strand.

I support two main charities. Navy SEAL/UDT Museum operates in Ft. Pierce, Florida. Please learn about this wonderful museum, all run by active and former SEALs and their friends and families, and who rely on public support, not that of the U.S. Government.

www.navysealmuseum.org

IF YOU GOT ANY CLOSER, YOU WOULD HAVE TO ENLIST

I also support Wounded Warriors, who tirelessly bring together the warrior as well as the family members who are just learning to deal with their soldier's condition and have nowhere to turn. It is a long path to becoming well, but I've seen first-hand what this organization does for its warriors and the families who love them. Please give what your heart tells you is right. If you cannot give, volunteer at one of the many service centers all over the United States. Get involved. Do something meaningful for someone who gave so much of themselves, to families who have paid the price for your freedom. You'll find a family there unlike any other on the planet.

www.woundedwarriorproject.org

CHAPTER 1

NAVY SEAL TUCKER Hudson woke up to his rosy-cheeked bride's snores. And she drooled, which had been one of the most remarkable things he'd discovered about her that first night they slept together. He watched the look on her face—totally engrossed in a dream of some kind, as spaced out as if she'd fallen asleep in a drunken stupor. Her plump upper lip folded and curled into a little sexy peak, showing a few of her front teeth. Brandy's hair scattered all over his chest, lovingly entangling him. Her right arm draped across his shoulder and hung free, her cheek pressed against his right upper chest.

It was deliciously hot and sticky next to her pink flesh. Carefully, he slipped his arm under the covers, reaching across his abdomen to pinch her right nipple.

She awoke with a squeak. He did all that for a squeak, that momentary tiny shock of terror before she realized he was ramping up to play with her as passionately as she wanted. And she usually liked it intense.

She moaned when his fingers searched below and found that little garden of delights. He lifted her knees then wrapped his arms around her waist and pulled her on top of him. She arched backward and gave him that view of her enormous breasts, which formed his growing erection.

"God, sweetheart, look at you. Look at us together," he said as he dug his fingers into her hips hoisting her above him long enough to position his shaft. She shuddered on the way down, her eyes rolling as he gently bounced her then clutched her breasts, hungry for their taste. Maybe it was his imagination, but she was bigger there than before the deployment, even though it was still very early in her pregnancy.

"You're gonna kill me seeing you all ripe and,"—he sucked in air as she formed a ring around his member at their joining—"big with my child."

"Oh, Tucker," she whispered as she stopped, and with her elbows squeezing her tits together, she allowed him to feel her flexing internal muscles.

She liked to get that first little one out of the way before they got into the heavy tussle that would leave them both breathless. And she could sustain her little ripple orgasm for long minutes until he was ready to explode.

He placed his thumb on her clit, and her eyes sprung open. "Suck me," she begged.

She really didn't have to ask.

THE MORNING SUN woke Tucker, blasting a laser over his brow, through a crack in the curtain. He'd go out and splurge for some blackout shades today, even though this was a rental. He was sad that with the upcoming deployment they wouldn't have time to do a proper house hunt and get Brandy situated before he had to leave. He was awaiting orders that could come any minute.

That part of his job really was the pits. It interrupted everything. Unlike a regular job where birthdays, holidays, and family events were sacred, his job ignored all those things and he was supposed to not let that upset him. He'd done it before with his first ten-year stint. But it was harder this go-around. When he was out, he spent the next ten years wishing he'd never left the Teams. Now he was back to square one, trying not to think about leaving Brandy again.

Except this time, he was newly married and expecting a child. And that made all the difference.

Brandy was probably awake and thinking too, because her breathing was surface and barely audible. He pondered yesterday's events. The day had started out okay but had turned into some gothic freak show during the evening with Brandy's discovery of a note his ex left in his jacket pocket. It surprised him how wounded she'd felt. He reminded himself to pay attention to that and not to see it as a defect in her character, for her past made her the lady she was today. She was kind, because she knew how it felt to be on the other side of cruel. She knew the difference between right and wrong with a backbone as strong as any he'd seen on the teams. That's why he loved her so much. If it meant he had to watch her insecurity about being his one and only, he'd do that. In spades. That was the key to her happiness.

It was also the key to his.

"Are you awake, Tucker?" she whispered as she snuggled into his neck.

His arm slipped around her waist again, as if it permanently belonged there. Her head tucked under his chin, and as he inhaled and exhaled, he took her body up and down with his rhythm.

"I am. Thinking about you, sweetheart." It was true.

"When do you think the call will come?"

"Have no idea. I'm guessing soon. We have to expect that, Brandy."

"I know." She propped herself up on her arms folded across his chest. One long finger traced down his slightly crooked nose, following over a scar he'd received from the last trip to Africa, and then across his lips, first the upper then the lower. She kissed him softly and examined them as she continued to trace.

"Say it." He knew she liked to tease like a little girl when she had something important on her mind.

She angled her head, as if to let the thoughts drain to somewhere she could speak about them. "I was thinking when you go, perhaps Dorie, Brawley and I could go on a road trip, if you think he's okay."

"I'd prefer that he go. I don't like the idea of you and Dorie on a road trip by yourselves."

"And yet we used to do it all the time."

"Before you were with me. Before Brawley. But you're both pregnant. She has a child, is getting ready to have twins, and Brawley's just recovering. Don't you think it's a little much?"

"You're probably right."

His fingers laced up her spine, enjoying the smoothness of her delicate skin. "I know you're looking for things to take your mind off the waiting. Maybe you and Christy could do more house searching?"

"But she's Kyle's better half, and she has the kids and so much responsibility while you and the Team are gone."

Kyle was their LPO, their Team leader, and as his wife, Christy Lansdowne was unofficially in charge of the wives, fiancés, and families.

"Maybe it will help her too. You could offer to babysit in exchange. She might appreciate that, since she does still work."

"I'll think about that." She smiled, staring down at his lips again. "Tucker, you have so many great ideas."

"I have another one I think you'll like," he whispered, raising up to meet her lips, then gently folding her beneath him in the bed.

CHAPTER 2

B RANDY LOOKED FORWARD to officially telling Dorie about their pregnancy and seeing how her best friend was coming along with her own. Most of the time since Tucker's return had been taken up with getting back into the routine of being home, assuming something of a "regular" life, which was never really that regular. Part of that was making sure Brawley had a station and job he could look forward to so Tucker wouldn't have to worry about him while he was gone again. So, under the dark cloud of that phone call letting them know the deployment was a go, they opted for a visit to Dorie and Brawley's home.

Jessica, Dorie and Brawley's toddler, was even more of a handful than she'd been a week ago when Brandy last saw her. She was tall for her age, taking after Brawley's side of the family, and not yet willowy like all the Hanks women with her baby fat still present. But she operated just like Brawley, like a tank crashing through life—breaking toys, furniture, and everything in her wake. Dorie looked exhausted, and Brandy noticed her center of gravity was changing with her showing belly.

Her beautiful friend pushed her blonde locks off her forehead, straightened her back with her right hand on her hip and blew out air with the stretch. "I keep thinking this is supposed to be the easy time. Imagine what it will be like when I have the three of them, all in diapers."

"You'll get lots of help, sweetie," Brandy said as she hugged Dorie.

"And then with Brawley. Well, it's like having a toddler, and a teenager to raise all at once, and me with a broken knee or foot or something."

"Now you're scaring me, Dorie. You mean being pregnant is a handicap?" Brandy gave her a wink.

Dorie stood taller and smiled. "Point taken. Not fair of me. It won't be like this for you. I apologize."

"Silly!" Brandy quipped back. She appreciated the comment and thanked her lucky stars she didn't have the same situation as her friend. "You're allowed to tell me whatever you like."

"Something tells me Tucker will be much more help around the house than Brawley is. My guy doesn't mind things in chaos, and he encourages Jessica to be fearless. She loves her daddy so much. Really cute to watch. My parenting style is slightly different."

"As it should be. After all, you're more delicate."

Dorie stared off to the side, giving a hard look at Brawley wrestling with Jessica in the backyard while Tucker stood beside them laughing. Brandy noted a slight frown. The snapshot of the two men, one a SEAL and one a former SEAL, "doing family" as Tucker called it, would forever be embedded in her memory. It was a reminder that life passed by at breakneck speed and that she should enjoy every moment for what it was. The future for these men and their families was always dangerous. But one thing was blazingly evident. They loved their families with a fierceness and loyalty unlike any other.

"Thank goodness I fell for him hard. Their bodies take all the scars, but they're in their element. We have the harder job, Brandy." She aimed her clear blue eyes toward her friend in an unwavering message of understanding they both shared. "We're the ones who pay the price."

A chill drifted over the room with Jessica's screams in the background. For the first time, Brandy saw fear resident in Dorie's eyes.

AFTER THE STARS came out and they had cleaned up the barbeque mess, Brawley put Jessica in his carry pack and the five of them drifted slowly down the beach.

Not much of the blush of the spectacular rose-colored sunset was left. Brandy's hand felt tiny gripped and protected by Tucker's huge paw. They swung their arms in the cadence of their gait, listening to the waves break on the shore and the call of late sea birds looking to settle down for the night. One or two small bonfires were lit, couples snuggling under blankets to stay warm, even though the breeze was mild. The ocean smoothed its way over the sand, erasing footsteps of long-forgotten travelers, rendering afternoon sandcastles into a melted mess.

Tucker drew his arm around her shoulders. "Are you warm enough?"

"I am now," she said as she leaned into his hulking frame.

"Watching Brawley and Jessica this afternoon, I was thinking about what our beach parties coming up would look like. I think we're going to have a water baby. We both love to swim so."

"I'm going to enroll her in swim classes as soon as her eyes can focus!" Brandy admitted, tugging on his tee shirt.

"Her, is it? You mean that? You think it's a girl?"

"I honestly have no idea. And I don't care. Maybe we could have a boy. Then he could marry Jessica and our families could be even more close."

She giggled as he squeezed her shoulder tight.

"Wouldn't that be something?" he whispered.

He continued walking, his head now downturned, watching their feet before the night erased them. "Tomorrow I'm going to the flea market with Brawley, and of course you can come too, if you want."

"This the big one or the auto one?"

"It's the big one."

"Of all the things you could do before you go overseas, why do that?"

He shrugged. "Just something normal."

She stopped in her tracks. Brawley and Dorie kept walking ahead. "*What?*" he asked.

"And just what is spending time with me, then?"

"Or," he began to stumble on his words, "I was about to say we could spend the whole day in bed. If it's safe for the baby."

"You were *not* going to say that." She watched him turn, then pull her to him.

"I just wanted to do something mindless. Our bedtime escapades are anything but mindless. I'm aware of every wiggle, shudder and moan. I am wide awake and loving every second of it, Brandy. You know that."

She felt herself blush from the top of her head all the way down to her toes. Her heart skipped a beat, and her palms grew hot. She touched his cheek. "It's the same for me, Tucker."

They ran to catch up to Brawley and Dorie. Jessica

had fallen asleep, and her little head was bobbing at an uncomfortable angle, so the four of them said good-night, and they returned to their respective houses.

It felt like the quiet before the storm.

CHAPTER 3

THE LARGE SATURDAY flea market drew crowds from all over Southern California. It was a mixture of cultures and languages, ages, sizes and personalities. The saying went, "If you can't find it at the flea market, you don't need it." Of course, one person's junk was another's treasure, and so the bartering and haggling going on rivaled any good bazaar in Marrakech and some of the open-air fruit and vegetable markets Tucker had visited in Europe.

Brawley was entranced with piles of slightly used and occasionally broken wooden toys he might be able to fix up for Jessica. That didn't interest Tucker in the slightest. But he was tempted by several large garden tools, mulchers, and chippers he could tinker with.

They met up with several other groups of Team guys who acted surprised to find each other but weren't, really. Wasting the day looking over discarded things was something many of the other brothers liked to do.

Fredo had bought a bag of flat soccer balls for the playground they were still sponsoring down at the old Catholic school they had converted to a neighborhood center. Cooper was giving him grief for not testing them first with a ball pump.

"They can be fixed, even if they do leak. Besides, doesn't make me feel so bad when they get 'borrowed', man. Right?" he told his lanky best friend.

"Still a waste of money," Cooper mumbled in return as he looked over a plastic bin of electrical cords, cables, and appliance chargers marked "One dollar each."

Fredo nodded toward Coop and squawked to Tucker. "You remember, Tuck? This is the guy who doesn't like to use more than one dryer sheet at a time. Who measures his dishwasher soap with a teaspoon?"

Tucker remembered their colossal fights back in the days when he was a newbie.

"It's not good for the dishwashers to have too much soap. Gunks up everything," Cooper said in his own defense.

Fredo couldn't be silenced. "He has to check his packets of ketchup by their expiration dates he has so many."

"I don't do that anymore. Libby—"

"Libby has made a regular guy out of him. But she

doesn't know he rents two storage spaces full of junk," Fredo continued.

"Like I said, I have enough parts to fix anything. And who is the one who fixed your blender? Who found all the handles Ali was using as projectiles for that sling shot Danny made for him?"

On and on it went. Tucker and Brawley and several others just fell in line behind them. Brawley found a vendor with handmade drums, and flutes, and crude instruments shaped and pounded out of coke cans. Another vendor was selling hand-loomed rugs from Central America and carved black lava figurines from Mexico.

At the first sign of a bicycle pump, Tucker sat and quietly demonstrated that about half of the balls did indeed leak. But they still fit into the net ball bag.

"This bag alone was worth the ten bucks," Fredo insisted.

Nearby, their group ran into Jackie Daniels and his two daughters. Jackie had been their Iraqi interpreter on missions Tucker had been on the first time around and over one thousand missions after Tucker had left. He'd fought bravely with the SEAL teams and was responsible for saving many lives, both US and Iraqi. In a narrow escape, he and his family had been allowed to immigrate to the US, and he'd just taken his Citizenship Oath. Jackie's code name was selected because of his love of whiskey, as well as an easy way to mask his real name to avoid retaliation on him and his family. Some of them still lived there.

"Jackie! So great to see you!" Tucker said as the two men embraced. Brawley, Fredo, and Coop, as well as several others, followed suit.

"Tucker, you're a braver man than I. No more for me." He lowered his voice to a whisper. "You can't get enough of all that shit over there?" Jackie said in his heavily accented but perfect English.

Tucker always admired Jackie most for his fondness for American swear words. He'd taught many of the men on Kyle's team how to swear in Pashtu during his early rites of diplomacy.

"Not over there. Hope we don't have to go back there. But yeah. I guess I just wasn't done. I'll know when that time comes."

"Yes, you will, my friend." He placed his arm on Tucker's shoulder then introduced the men to his two daughters, who dutifully looked downcast and wouldn't touch any of the Americans. Both wore their headscarves, an odd addition to their over-worn faded jeans and high-top tennis shoes in red, white, and blue. Tucker guessed if Jackie wore shorts, his would also be with stars and stripes, just like the ones most guys on Team 3 donned every day.

"Got myself married and a little one on the way,

too," Tucker informed him, holding his belly as if he was the pregnant one.

"That will make a real man out of you, Tucker."

"She's trying real hard."

Brawley barked the understatement, addressing Jackie's daughters. "Your dad's a hero, ladies. You gotta know that."

The group burst out in Hooyahs like a colony of sea lions, attracting attention from the flea market crowd surrounding them. The girls shyly tucked behind Jackie but smiled. Tucker knew Jackie was too high profile to continue with the adulation in public, for his own safety.

"So what brings you out here? What could you possibly need in all this junk?" asked Fredo, who scowled when Cooper pointed to his bag of soccer balls. The Latino SEAL leaned in. "Coop wants to find a good deal on another Babemobile," he finished off with a whisper, which earned him a major punch in the arm from his Nebraska best bud.

Jackie laughed at all of them. "You guys never change, do you?" He turned to his girls. "Hands." He demonstrated by cupping his hands over his own ears and watched his daughters mimic the motion. He addressed the men, "I miss all the shit-talk. I've almost forgotten how to swear." He grinned, showing off his white teeth. "It does my heart fuckin' good!"

Jackie nodded to the girls, who removed their hands.

"Heard you took the Oath. Welcome to the good old US of A," said Coop as he shook Jackie's hand.

"You bet. Very proud. A very proud day for me, indeed."

"You still haven't answered my question," asked Fredo.

Jackie gave a respectful gaze around the open-air market, examining faces, stalls, piles of goods, and plastic bins full of everything imaginable. He nodded and then gave his answer. "The first thing I did when I came to America was to take the girls to go buy a hamburger and milkshake with my crisp new American dollars. I'd dreamt about doing this my whole life."

The group around him remained silent. Even his girls listened with rapt attention.

"The next thing I did was to come here, to these bazaars. I wanted to see what you Americans discard. Many of these things that are being sold off or given away I'd never seen before. I know some people think I'm crazy. I ask them, 'What's this?' and they look at me like I'm from Mars. I've learned so much about your country by looking at flea markets and the people who come here."

Tucker examined his shoes. Several other men cleared their throats or adjusted their shirts.

Jackie added, "I first learned about your culture from you SEALs. You guys did a terrible thing, igniting the fires of freedom in my soul but giving me a very warped sense of what it's like to live here. Thought I'd get a little more perspective. Get the *whole* picture."

No one seemed to have an answer to Jackie's heartfelt comments. Tucker knew the rest of the team felt just like he did. The cost of freedom was very dear. But looking into the face of this brave Iraqi man and his beautiful family, Tucker knew the price was worth every drop of shed blood. They'd all do it over and over again, until they couldn't. But they'd never forget what they'd tried to do and how they served.

CHAPTER 4

THE CALL CAME in at midnight. Late night interruptions were always jarring, but Brandy was adjusting to the unexpected, and this call wasn't exactly a surprise. She'd been in a deep sleep when she heard Tucker's whispers as he cupped the cell to his ear and tried to get out of bed without disturbing her.

Tucker confirmed what she already knew. They were going to deploy in two days. At least she had two days with him. It wasn't enough, but she'd make it stretch just like the rest of the month felt when Tucker's check had been nearly spent.

"So it's back to Nigeria, then?" she dared to ask as Tucker slipped in to spoon behind her.

"Mrs. Hudson, that's on a need to know basis," he said as he kissed her shoulder and then settled back into the pillows. "But the answer to that question is yes and no."

She pondered this briefly then fell asleep with

Tucker's oversized hand palming her belly.

Next morning, Tucker took them down to the harbor to have breakfast and walk along the pier, examining the boats, both large and small. Crews who took tourists out on the water were at work early washing and polishing their crafts. A variety of music blended in the early morning moist air—classical, reggae, and some oldies rock.

"Maybe we should take your dad's money and just buy a boat and sail away, never come back, Brandy," Tucker said as he pulled her jacket collar up around her ears.

"I'm not going to have a baby on a deserted island somewhere or on a boat in the middle of the Pacific without good medical equipment and staff."

"Hey? What am I?"

She smiled, never passing up the opportunity to tease him about his work. "You're good at removing limbs and stopping the blood spurting everywhere, but have you ever delivered a baby?" She looked up at his expression of surprise.

"Why yes, I have."

"You never told me that."

He shrugged. "Part of the medical course at Bragg. And first tour I delivered twins in Afghanistan to one of the village girls. We had to improvise."

"I'll bet. Honestly, I never knew this. Did it make

you nervous?"

"Hell no," he said as they entered the diner and were shown to their table. "In Oregon, we had animals. I'm actually better at hatching chicks."

Brandy frowned as they sat. "Don't chicks hatch on their own?"

"Yes, and so do puppies, goats, horses, and little pink Brandy and Tucker babies."

"Good to know. Geez, I hope ours isn't born with a shell."

"Very funny." He grabbed her hands and held them from across the table. "But I agree with you. We want the best. And being alone on a remote island might sound more romantic than it would be. It's one thing to put myself at risk, but now that someone else is coming to live with us, well, that's a different story."

Tucker dropped his eyes, deep in thought. He watched their fingers entwined on the wooden tabletop, his large thumb rubbing against hers. She waited, now recognizing the signs of something he wanted to say he was having trouble putting into words.

"When I was on the Teams last time, our deployments were regular. We worked up for it, trained, retrained, and studied what the job was. Then we went over, and usually, the length of deployment was about equal to the workup. Afterwards, we'd have that amount of time to be at home, or go to a specialty course, or heal, depending on how we came home."

His brown eyes stared deep into hers, and for a second, a shudder came over her. It was part excitement and part fear. Her pulse quickened. She loved Tucker's intensity, even when it was bad news.

"Now, things have changed. Things are active all over the world. It isn't in one or two theaters. It's all over the world. We used to train Special Forces from other countries, kind of the "Show and Tell" brigade. We were supposed to demonstrate why we're so awesome, and, to be honest, part of it was propaganda so other bad guys wouldn't fuck with us."

"Okay," she said, drawing it out, answering his focus with a smile. "Where is this going, Tucker?"

"So now we don't always get much notice. That means sometimes the training is limited. We go over more often, I'm being told, and this is what I wanted to speak to you about."

"About what?"

"Well, we'll be going over to those hot spots more frequently. Maybe not staying as long, but more missions. Perhaps more time away from home than I originally thought. I wanted to prepare you for the possibility that you could go into labor when I cannot come home and be with you. They try to work it out, but it might not be possible, honey."

Now she understood what he was trying to tell her.

"I think I understand. What you're telling me is that the SEAL Teams don't give you paternity leave."

He chuckled. "That would be the day. If I was an officer, perhaps. But not for a regular Joe like me."

She leaned across the table and nearly collided with their food and coffee. After the waitress left, she answered him. "Tucker, there isn't anything regular about you. Everything about you is *supersized,* including your heart. I'm going along with whatever it is that you want to do. It's all good."

"So you won't miss me?"

"I didn't say that," she said as she threw a napkin at him which hit him in the face.

"You'll pay for that," he growled.

"I was counting on it." She felt her cheeks turn bright red.

CHRISTY LANSDOWNE CALLED on their way home, telling Brandy that she found a house she wanted them to look at, if they had the time.

"How can we buy a house when you're overseas?" mumbled Brandy, her arms crossed.

"DocuSign."

"Excuse me?"

"DocuSign. I did it for one of my deployments. I even got a car loan once that way."

"You mean electronic signature. Is that safe?"

"Depends on where we are."

"You said yes-or-no-Africa. I meant to ask you what the heck you meant, Tucker."

His GPS directed them to a little green two-story house that was taller than it was wide, tucked behind dense gardens and several brand new or majorly remodeled mansions. The house address was on Flora Avenue. He knew he'd get a load from the Team about that. But then, Cooper lived on Apricot, so what the heck.

Tucker shut off the truck's motor and glanced down the street both directions then eyed the home carefully. "Kind of cute. I like that it's off the road. And only what three blocks to the beach?"

"Oh, no, you don't. Tell me."

"Tell you what?"

"You know. The mission."

"We're going to the Canaries off the west coast of Africa. Island cluster that's part of Spain. Definitely feels more Spanish than African. And it's a lot safer too."

"Wow. Sounds exotic." Brandy noticed Christy's car pull up in front of them. She was wearing a light blue suit, which looked stunning with her blonde hair and athletic build. Christy motioned for them to follow her.

Tucker continued. "It's nice. Great vacation spot

for Brits and others from Europe. I've been there once before, briefly. Come on. Let's go see the house."

Tucker helped her from the truck.

Before they reached Christy, he added, "Mum's the word, Brandy. We don't talk about this in front of Christy. I'm not supposed to tell."

"Roger that, Mr. Hudson."

"Oh, you have a smart mouth today, Mrs. Hudson. I know just what you can do with that mouth a little later."

Tucker took hold of her hand, and before she could give a snappy retort, he pulled her down a narrow path through lush foliage about ten feet behind Christy.

"So one of the ladies in the office listed this just this morning, but it hasn't been put on MLS yet. We're the first to see it." Christy beamed. "Now prepare yourself, because I've been told it's a little plain, nothing done to it in like sixty years. It might be pretty bad. I suspected so when Danielle told me the listing price. Don't be mad, okay?"

"But geez, Christy, it's nearly a million dollars," gasped Tucker.

"But we're totally cool with it," said Brandy. "Thanks for thinking of us."

"Is it vacant?" asked Tucker.

"The owner has been living in a rest home for over twenty years. Family members have kept the jungle at bay and, I think, kept the house clean. But all his things are supposedly still in there. He never got to go back home."

Brandy felt sad for the owner.

"I know it's at the upper limits of your price range. I just hope that the work it needs doesn't blow it out of the park," Christy continued and then opened the front door.

It felt like they'd just stepped back in time about forty years. The kitchen had real wood cabinets— knotty pine—with vinyl countertops trimmed in stainless steel edging. Brandy felt instantly in love with the charm. As she walked down the hall and heard the hardwood floors squeak, she giggled. "I love that sound!"

Tucker and Christy exchanged glances.

The bathrooms were lined in blue and black four-inch tiles, trimmed in diamond-shaped edging pieces with art deco designs. One bath had a real porcelain tub and an etched glass medicine cabinet like the one Brandy remembered from her grandmother's home. The other bathroom, the master, was totally tiled in the same blue and black colors, but with a tiny stall shower and a doorway barely large enough for Tucker to step in.

"We'll get a bid on what it would cost to remodel these. This will never work for you guys," said Christy.

"So if there are two bedrooms downstairs, including the master, what's upstairs?"

Christy's eyes sparkled. "Just wait. Now be careful."

The stairway was way too narrow but passable. At the top landing they came upon a great room the size of the house footprint with wall-to-wall model trains. It was a replica of a tiny village, complete with a main street of Victorian houses, a post office, and several stores that looked like they were from the early nineteen hundreds.

"This is amazing," whistled Tucker.

"His daughter told their Realtor that he was a member of several model train clubs. This village, of course, doesn't go with the house. It's being left to the heirs and probably will go in a train museum somewhere. But isn't it fun?"

"What would you put up here?" asked Brandy.

"A gym," said Tucker.

"A new master suite with nursery?" Christy added.

"We could convert it to a separate unit, Tucker. Make it into a duplex. We'd have to add a kitchen and bathroom, add outside stairs, but what do you think?"

Christy interrupted her. "Great idea. I'm not sure the zoning will allow it but definitely worth asking."

Tucker was focusing on the detail of the village, studying the miniature locomotive and cars. "If I ever brought Coop here, he'd never leave," he mumbled.

Brandy walked along the four walls, since the stairway came up through the middle of the room. She noticed the ring of windows, which would let in sunlight all day long. "I could paint here. Tucker, you could write." Brandy's voice trailed off softly as she luxuriated in the visualizations coming at her so fast it was hard to remember them all.

Christy turned and faced Tucker. "You write?"

He shrugged without answering. He rolled his right shoulder and searched the room as if he were looking for a vacant desk. "I've been keeping a journal, but yes, thought I'd tell some tall tales of danger, adventure, and valor." He rolled his eyes and winked at Christy.

"I think that's really cool," said Christy. "Good for you."

"And not a word to Kyle, either. They'd tease me to hell and back."

"Your secret is safe with me. A hobby room, then, is it?" said Christy.

"That's it."

"You think they'd allow some seller financing?" Brandy asked. "I don't want to use up all Dad's money and not have anything left for the remodel this would require."

"I can ask," said Christy. "But if you're interested, we'd have to jump on it right away. Good news for you is that you've already sold your father's home, so you can be a non-contingent sale. With fifty percent down, you qualify for a four hundred-thousand-dollar loan, right?"

"Yes," answered Brandy. She was trying to get Tucker's attention.

"What do you think, Tuck?" asked Christy.

"You know we're leaving day after tomorrow, right?" he mumbled, still focusing on the model trains.

"Yes. That will present some problems, but I think we can work it out, if you like the house. There are only a handful of houses on Coronado under a million—I think less than five. There might be multiple offers if you wait too long."

Brandy hung on every movement Tucker made. Her mind was filling with ideas. She thought about removing some of the shrubbery in front and expanding the yard space, since the lot was so small compared to the surrounding homes. After a few silent minutes, she noted Tucker wasn't making eye contact.

She waited until he looked up at her. His eyes betrayed something he was trying to hide. At last a smile drew across his face. "You always grab the first thing that comes along?" he whispered, following it with a little smirk. He was too damn sexy for his own good.

"I know a good thing when I see one," she replied. "And, yes I go for it. I grab it and never let go."

CHAPTER 5

TEAM 3 GATHERED in their building on base so the mission could be explained. They were scheduled to leave at Zero-Four-Hundred the next morning for their mission to the Canary Islands off the western coast of Africa.

Tucker's bags were already packed at home. He settled between Coop and DeWayne Huggles, their language specialist from Mississippi.

Kyle began the presentation before he turned the floor over to the young State Department Special Agent, who would be accompanying their group. Kelly Fielding looked like she had just graduated from high school, but Kyle told them she'd already worked in Africa for nearly eight years and had a master's in International Relations with an emphasis on the African continent. He also told them she was fluent in about a dozen languages.

Huggles swore under his breath. "This is going to

be fucked."

Tucker knew many of the men already started out with a bias against the "brains" in the State Department who often overruled action with diplomacy. But when their lead was a woman, as well, it made for a double strike. He knew the SEALs weren't necessarily there to fix the problem but to get everyone out safely when it became one.

Tucker whispered back, "Give her a chance, man."

Huggles' eyebrows nearly got lost in his scalp, his eyes wide with feigned shock.

When Kelly began to speak, half the back row barked that they couldn't hear her voice, so she repeated her introduction much louder than her normal timbre, and it made her face turn red from the stress. She was probably nervous as hell, Tucker thought.

The problem with doing missions when females were on hand was that half the younger men would need to have everything explained to them all over again, since the sight of such a beautiful, red-headed peach-skinned creature made their brains malfunction. It was simply a lack of blood to the right organ, having been diverted elsewhere.

Tucker wasn't worried for himself, even though he could admit she was attractive as hell. It was the violation of their Team building, their private space, that worried him the most. It rarely happened, so this was a big deal, according to his superiors. He was used to the cold smell of firepower, explosives, and metal, not the exotic floral scent of her perfume. It somehow diluted the man-cave, tradition and, besides that, felt all wrong.

"Thank you, Chief Lansdowne," she began. She took a moment to scan the room, making eye contact with everyone sitting before her.

Kyle took his seat in the front row and crossed his legs.

"I'm familiar with this group who managed to smuggle Jenna out of Nigeria. And I also know her family," began Agent Fielding. "Her father's a well-known philanthropist in the Northwest. Although this is a joint State and Special Forces operation, we've been authorized to let you know no expense will be spared. We believe she has been trafficked, and the group perhaps does not know about her famous and very wealthy family. We want to keep it that way."

Tucker didn't like the idea that special treatment would be happening, which was just another way of saying he and all the other team guys were more at risk than usual. Secrets were never good. They always cost lives of the "little" people.

"It looks like she was sold to a Dutch billionaire who does a fair amount of business with the raiding Nigerian militant gangs. He gets drugs and conflict diamonds from them and, in exchange, sells the militants guns. He's been on the State Department's radar for about three years now. Much of his business is disguised as building roads and wind generators, which he claims he doesn't do for profit. We know otherwise, of course. There have been rumors he's begun to dip his toe into the lucrative human trafficking business."

As the agent continued, her voice got lower, and she became laser-focused on identifying pictures of various characters projected on the wall of their buildings, explaining who the organization was and how it operated.

In the lull after her presentation, Cooper asked, "So where is this place where they're holding her, or do you know?"

"Oh, we know," Agent Fielding answered. She threw up another slide of an enormous white building that looked more like a commercial lab than a residence. It was heavily fortified, a regular fortress guarded by roughly one hundred men, she told them.

Kyle uncrossed his legs and sat up straight. "The militia groups may not know who her father is, but what's the chance this billionaire slave trader doesn't know?" he asked.

"Well, the State Department has not allowed him to obtain a US visa. Most of his trade is with Europe,

United Kingdom, and South America. I'd say of all the countries of the world; he knows least about the US. But it's always possible, Chief."

"So what's the plan for getting into the compound?" asked a heavily-accented voice from the rear. Tucker recognized him immediately. Several other SEALs turned around to confirm Sven Tolar had indeed made it to San Diego, and, apparently, would be tagging along.

That was great news.

The agent deferred to their LPO for the tactical details. But while Kyle explained his plan, Tucker noticed the room's energy, with the addition of Sven to the Team, had suddenly exploded in chatter and crosstalk. One by one, members shook Sven's hand and then stood next to him in a group while they listened. For the first time, Tucker was filled with happy anticipation. He turned to the frowning Huggles.

"What do you know? I actually think we have a chance here."

AFTER THE MEETING, Tucker greeted several men he hadn't seen in months, as well as Sven Tolar, the retired Norwegian Specialist they'd met on the previous mission to Nigeria. Although he didn't know Sven back then, he remembered their grueling joint training operations back some ten years or more. Tucker always had a great deal of admiration for these men, considering them to be the best-trained team in survival tactics, no matter the weather. They'd been legendary for fighting the Nazis, the Russians and anyone else who thought they could defeat their much smaller numbers. Tucker had learned they could live in snow caves virtually undetected for months at a time.

"What a huge surprise and a boon for us all," Tucker said as they briefly embraced.

"I said I'd look you up."

"Well, damn, didn't know it would be this way. Nonetheless, glad to have you aboard. Are you part of the intel here?"

"Nope. Just a private contractor. I guess I got listed on some asset sheet," Sven added.

Tucker knew that was probably Kyle's doing. Kyle had extensive files and contact information on good men they'd worked with in the past outside the SEAL community.

"How's your friend?" Sven spoke softly. "I don't see him here."

Tucker took a deep breath at the mention of Brawley. "Nah, he's retired. Going to begin being a BUD/S instructor until he can get his twenty in." He looked down at his feet and then up to connect with Sven's deep penetrating eyes. "It was a close one."

"I'll say it was. We've lost a few too. They would

just walk off into the forest, and we never see them again."

It broke Tucker's heart to hear of a warrior, a man of action who chose to end his life. Suicides were on the rise in the military, even on the Teams.

"I guess we can't save them all," Tucker whispered.

Several other men joined their circle, ending the conversation. Tucker said his farewells and headed for home.

His happy mood had turned, and he wondered about that. It was a good thing that they'd have Sven's help. This wasn't going to be the kind of deployment that would be months long. They were to go in, grab the nurse, and get out. So why was he so blue all of a sudden?

Tucker thought about the house they were trying to buy, and how happy Brandy had been when they found out their offer had been accepted. But he wondered if it all was too soon. Should he take one step at a time? Should they have the baby first, learn how to be good parents, then take on the financial responsibility of the house payments? Being a SEAL was more rewarding than being a regular Navy guy, but he still didn't make nearly enough money to own a close to million-dollar house. He was having second thoughts about allowing her to talk him into it. And his pride was a little bit dusted up that it was Brandy's money—money she got from her father. Tucker had always paid for everything with his own funds, earned with his own hands.

You're thinking too much, Tucker. You've got to keep your head on straight. Concentrate on what's ahead of you. Be grateful for what you have.

That was it. He'd not been grateful enough lately. He was going to be a father. He was married to a wonderful woman. He'd successfully gotten his buddy home safely and seen to it that he was positioned right for the best possible results. His family was going to plant roots, own something that would keep them close to the beach, ensconced in the community he loved.

Next time he opened his journal, he was going to write about that—all the good things coming to him, not the things that were at risk.

But the thought of a man walking into the woods to purposely end his life still chilled him. It had happened to Brawley. He hoped, if it ever happened to him, he'd recognize the signs in time.

CHAPTER 6

BRANDY KNEW TUCKER should be home early from the meeting, not have a pitstop at the Scupper. But when she heard his truck, she was relieved. It was going to be their last night together, and he had to be at the base by three.

"Hey there," he said as he tossed his keys and grabbed her for a smothering bearhug. "Wanna miss dinner and fool around until I have to go?" His eyes sparkled as that little smirk crept across his lips.

"I could be up for that. Anything you need to do first?"

"Think we could take a shower? Then I won't have to shower in the morning."

"That sounds nice," she said as that familiar tingle tickled all the way down her spine. "But maybe you'll be too hot and sweaty and—"

His big mouth covered hers, making words impossible. His hands were already digging into the top of her pants, and then those pants were down at her ankles.

"I think I'd like to taste you a bit first, maybe," he said through his teeth, not giving her a chance for a reply. "Then I might want to slather some of that lemony gel all over your body so I can have a nice, lasting image of what I'll be coming home to."

When his fingers breached the elastic of her panties and penetrated her core, she inhaled sharply and pressed herself into his hand, raising one thigh to rest on his hip. He quickly disposed of her panties, kneeled, slipped her knee over his shoulder, and licked his lips as he examined her sex. His quiet deliberation and his slow movements had her breathless with anticipation. Finally, his tongue was on her clit, making its way inside her opening.

She gripped his shoulder with one hand while the other sifted and tugged at his hair. Her pelvis quivered as his tongue explored and set her on fire. He took his time, giving tiny love bites extending into the soft tissues of her upper thigh. His thumbs pressed as his lips drank from her and had her begging for a night of lovemaking that would never end.

Maybe it was the sweetness of knowing that he'd be gone for a few weeks—hopefully only a few days. Maybe it was because she was more sensitive now because she was carrying his child. But whatever it was, the fire in her belly grew, filling her with cruel need. She was completely his.

He gently rose, taking her hand, and led her to the shower where he stripped. Her breathing was ragged, and her desire for him so great, she hungrily stared at his beautiful, chiseled body with his enormous cock teasing her. She didn't remember how she got undressed, but when she stepped into the warm spray, his arms were about her, his mouth on her mouth, pressing deep, moving her to the slick tiles at her back. Effortlessly, he hoisted her up, hands under her thighs as she rocked against his hips. He bent his knees and angled himself and then pushed his way deep inside her.

She nearly fainted. There was so much she wanted to say, but he had total command over her mouth. He begged for her hands on his shaft. He drank her moans. He kissed her neck. She felt the hard muscles of his chest press her such that she could hardly breathe. Her hands slid up his lower back, feeling his huge muscles deliciously ripple as he thrust hard and deep, repeating and picking up the intensity until her bones were made rubber.

After several minutes he quickly shifted. He held her under the spray and, as her orgasm peaked, he spent inside her and then stroked her back. His chest heaved and then let out an enormous sigh, but he held her still, lovingly brushing down her shoulders and arms, finding her mouth and placing soft nurturing kisses there. At last he moved from side to side, cuddling her in his enormous arms as the water covered them both.

They didn't speak the rest of the evening, and Brandy knew there was so much to say that it would take weeks to get it all out. But she didn't want to spoil the sacred night. It was that little pretense, like they'd be separated forever and this would be the last time they could make love, making them so desperate for each other. Gallows sex, it had been called in one of her romance books.

She was filled, consumed with him, loving him in the flesh here and now, because time was so precious and unpredictable.

SHE HAD THOUGHT she was still awake, still dreaming about his powerful body, when she felt his kiss whisper over her skin, "Don't wake up. Don't open your eyes. It's time."

But she couldn't help it and opened them anyway, giving him a tug as he was trying to stand up. He took her with him, squeezed her body and then settled her back down on the bed.

"Hold that thought, Brandy. I'll be back before you know it. Maybe the next time you wake up."

She smiled through her tears. "I vowed I wouldn't cry, and I'm so sorry, Tucker."

"Honey, don't ever apologize for showing me how much you'll miss me. Don't ever apologize for that." He kissed her and then left the bedroom.

Naked, still breathing hard from what she felt like was hours of uninterrupted sex, she listened to the front door close behind him and the roar of Brawley's truck pulling out of the driveway.

She was filled with wicked thoughts like running outside and begging him to come back, of making a scene, but she tucked herself in the wet and warm sheets that smelled of him, rubbed her belly softly and allowed sleep to take over.

THAT AFTERNOON, BRANDY signed the confirmation to the escrow instructions for their future home over at Christy's house. Her beautiful realtor was a mess just like Brandy was. She could see the traces of tears, and she knew that, even after what must have been a hundred missions, it still affected Christy the same way.

Her kids were playing in the backyard as she handed Brandy a tall glass of ice water. Even in sweats with her hair up in a scrunchie, Christy Lansdowne was one of the most beautiful women she'd ever met. She had the kind of classic beauty that Dorie had.

"Now, when we get time to sign the final papers, you'll have to get your power of attorney out so you can sign for him."

"Yes, I understand." It had been one of the things required when she married Tucker. She had the durable power of attorney for illness, finances, everything. The Navy required all these things in case of the unthinkable. And for good reason, too. It would minimize the further pain of losing a loved one to have the "affairs"—meaning the things one had to do with the rest of her life—in order.

And everything else could be done with DocuSign, everything but a grant deed.

"So, I'll order a pest inspection on Monday. I'll get a home inspection contractor out there, and I think we should get one for the roof too, what do you think?" Christy re-tied her hair up atop her head.

"That sounds good. You have people you like to use?"

"Yes. But you can choose."

Brandy had some poor experiences with the inspections for her father's home and didn't want to repeat that. "No, the guy that the buyers used was horrible. Remember?"

"Oh yes, the old guy who wouldn't go under the house and called out tiny rips in the window screens? We didn't get a choice, but don't worry. We'll not use them."

"Great."

Noise was coming from the backyard, and Christy was out the back door in a flash. Brandy heard a major scolding going on just before she returned to the kitchen.

"We have a couple of their friends over. It helps the kids to keep their minds off the fact that daddy is gone."

Brandy understood the wisdom of Christy's words. There was so much she needed to learn. Here she thought buying a house with Tucker being overseas was difficult, yet families did this sort of thing every day, with kids, illness, and all sorts of things going on at the same time. Brandy and Tucker's life was rather uncomplicated in comparison.

"You're so great with those kids and with all the Team wives too. And you work. I don't see how you do it."

"I did it just like you're going to do it, Brandy. Bit by bit. I had great teachers. Kyle being a leader meant that came with the territory." Christy stopped, took a sip of her water. "You know, Kyle thinks Tucker has some potential as a leader. Have you two ever considered sending him to OCS?"

"He thinks he's too old. No. I don't think he wants that. But he loves being one of the ones the Team guys, especially the younger ones, look up to."

"It's the healing side of him, the medic side. I can see that," said Christy.

She was right. There wasn't anyone else who could have helped save Brawley but Tucker. "He's one of the guys you can count on. Always."

"Then we're all lucky to have him. Hang onto him, Brandy."

"Oh, I intend to!"

They both laughed.

After she left, Brandy wandered through several large home improvement stores, looking at counter-tops, cabinets, and appliances. She picked up brochures for window coverings and paint samples.

She stopped by her favorite art store and purchased some new water color pencils and acrylics, along with several new paper tablets and two canvases. She'd taken the time to select colors she remembered from the house, as well as the color of the blue and white surf, and the beach. She wanted to do some sketches of color schemes for a new kitchen and a decent-sized bathroom. Making love in the shower was almost a routine for them now. That tiny one would have to go.

Before she returned home, she stopped by the house they had in contract. With the memory of Tucker's kisses still fresh on her skin and her sex swollen from all the lovemaking they'd done last night, she slowly walked down the green path toward the front door.

This would be the home they'd raise their baby in. This exciting new chapter was the start of something bigger. She was ready for it all. She wanted to remember every sight and smell of it all.

She had thought her life had started when she met Tucker that New Year's Eve at Dorie and Brawley's wedding. But this was the real start. This is where it would all begin.

CHAPTER 7

THE HARDEST PART of any trip was always the transport across the Atlantic. They usually rode in a troop transport plane that lacked any amenity but a bathroom, and some didn't even have those, which made a ten-hour flight even longer. But this sleek jet had been chartered, and Tucker knew it had something to do with the girl's father.

So far, so good.

There were ten of them who went this time, a smaller number than those who went to Nigeria last month. It was thought that the extraction would be quick, just like some of those snatch and grabs they used to do in his early Afghanistan deployments— before the rules of engagement had changed, when you could actually do those. Now those poor guys had to practically post it on the front page of the Times and then try to go in by "surprise." These days, you had to get permission for something you knew you weren't going to do, so you could execute Plan B, which had been the real plan all along. Or so Tucker had been told by some of the older guys who remained in after Tucker left.

He took a window seat, placing his bag on the spot next to him. He was hoping to be able to get his large frame comfortable and then catch up on some of those erotic dreams he knew he'd have. He wanted to imagine what it would have been like to extend their lovemaking session another three hours or more. Nothing wrong with the way it went, though.

Absolutely nothing fuckin' wrong. Last night was perfect.

One by one, the rest of the Team wandered down the aisle. Several people noticed his bag, taking up the seat space, but most just kept walking past him. Kelly Fielding hesitated for a second, but when Tucker didn't move his bag, she kept going.

Behind her was Sven, who whispered in her ear, "Sorry, darlin', but he was saving it for me. Hope your feelings aren't charred."

Tucker actually saw that Sven was kind of sweet on the Special Agent, which was a big surprise. He didn't like himself for trying to be too wary of a woman on the mission, but he was grateful for Sven's save. Personal politics was never Tucker's strong point, unless he was the teacher, of course.

He pulled his bag off the seat and let it hit the floor with a thud.

"How about we do this like adults, Tucker." Sven picked up the pack and placed it in the overhead bin—also something not usually found on their transport plane. Sven loaded his pack up next to it.

"Thanks, man. I guess I wasn't very nice." Tucker turned his head around to see if Agent Fielding could hear him. She was way to the back of the plane.

"I was saving you from pissing off the most important person on this plane," said Sven as he sunk down hard in the seat.

Tucker was shocked. "Excuse me?"

Sven lowered his voice until Tucker could barely hear. "She's the nurse's sister-in-law."

"No shit? Don't you think Kyle should have mentioned it?"

"I don't think he knows."

Tucker let his head hit the back of the seat. The take-off instructions were announced, and within minutes, they'd taxied and were in the air. Tucker looked down with pride at the Navy's fleet, some of the finest ships and equipment in the world and the men who were dedicated to using every gadget to keep the world safe. Being a Fleet Commander was like running a small foreign country but paid far less.

So this was going to be another mission with secrets. They were walking into something and even though they were to put their lives on the line, they were still not good enough to be made aware of all the little minute details that could blow the whole thing sky high.

"Question for you. Are we the hired help, or working for Uncle Sam?"

"Depends on who you ask. If you asked her father-in-law, he'd say the POTUS works for him. But I think he exaggerates a bit." Sven scrunched up his nose with that last comment.

Tucker searched for Kyle and found him up front with Cooper and Fredo and several of the others. Par for the course, Kyle wasn't letting them sleep, but laying out maps and showing them pictures, while the person with all the information was sitting in the back near the bathroom. He started grinding his teeth.

"Don't even think about it," grumbled Sven.

"I have to tell him. He'd do the same for me."

"When the time comes. When we have to. Right now, we need him raw. You don't know Kelly like I do," he said as he wiggled his eyebrows up and down.

"Oh, really?" Tucker said with a grin.

"Well, almost. I like to move slower than the ladies. You'd be surprised what the result gets you."

Tucker knew what he was talking about. It was exactly what happened with him and Brandy. If he strung it out and then let her take the lead, he was in for a mind-blowing experience.

Sven chuckled. "I thought maybe she liked ladies. So I asked her, and she took it on herself to prove me wrong."

"Son of a bitch. I rescind your invitation to visit us in San Diego. Consider yourself disinvited."

They both had a big laugh over that one. Tucker was pulling down tears he laughed so loud.

"You Viking assholes have some moves, I'll give you that."

"We have to. We're smaller than you Yanks. When have you ever heard a lady boast of balling a Norwegian? But how about an American SEAL? I'm just trying to catch up. My heritage is on the line."

Tucker found he liked Sven more each time he was around him. He was smart as well as good at his job. Not good at his job and stupid like Brawley was. He'd always thought the SEALs attracted men who had major flaws and needed their demons excised. The type of guys who could defend a whole village and then go home and have a salami sandwich and a beer and fall asleep in front of the TV. Those guys would wake up someday broke and alone, hardly speaking to their grown kids, and after they were out, they never were the same. Sven's guys could probably do their jobs and then go back to being preschool teachers and think nothing of it.

American SEALs did the things everyone else was too damned scared to do, and for good reason. That was the real payoff for them.

"So I'm surmising you and Kelly spent some time together in Paris, then?"

"Actually, I visited her in the Canaries. We're the ones responsible for the surveillance."

"Now I'm really interested. Between the time we left Nigeria and now, you hooked up with Kelly on the Canary Islands—"

"We hung out in Morocco too. Spent a couple of days on Capri. That was strictly fun."

"So you posed as a couple? Taking pictures?"

"Yup," Sven said as he nodded.

"Drinking wine and wandering around the streets at all hours of the day or night?"

"Yessir! That's exactly what we did."

"A couple?"

"I already said we did. We made it convincing too."

"I'll just bet you did."

"And the nurse's dad, he knew about this?" Tucker asked.

"He paid for the trip."

"But—Sven, I don't want to ask you how you arranged all that. I'm assuming Kelly's married to his son?"

"*Was.*"

Tucker looked straight ahead. "I'm not sure I want to know the rest of this story, Sven. You're kind of creeping me out."

Sven shrugged. "There's a simple and perfectly logical explanation, Tucker. Kelly's husband, the old man's son, and Jenna's brother, died of an overdose two years ago."

"And he thinks this Dutch guy had something to do with it?"

"Indirectly. It doesn't wrap up too pretty like that. But, Tucker, he's already lost one son to drugs. Now his daughter is sold into some kind of sex slavery. If you had all the money in the world and no family to leave it to, what would you do with it?"

"I'd go find the bad guys and make them pay."

"Exactly. And if your daughter-in-law is a Special Agent working for the State Department and has contacts and you have some cash for some fundraising parties for the President, don't you think an accommodation could be worked out?"

Tucker was amazed Kelly had spoken to them and kept a straight face. She was good. Really good. But the situation still bothered him, and he had to bring it up.

"Sven, our Teams aren't a private for-hire group that go in and do things for influential friends of the present administration."

"Apparently, they don't put that in your textbooks. There have been world wars fought exactly for that purpose, my friend. But make no mistake, these are the real bad guys. And if they could, and with enough time and money they'll achieve it, they'd destroy any Western nation who tries to interrupt their income stream. Maybe I see it differently because we're sort of neutral. Not really neutral, but we don't have the money to go overseas and start or end wars. We give token support to the good guys, we hope."

Tucker pondered this. *How did they decide where to send the Teams in the first place?*

"We're helping one man get his daughter back. We're helping to interfere with some bad elements preying on innocents and American interests in Africa, obstructing, among other things, their importation of drugs that are killing off your American children. I think it's a fair trade-off, Tucker. Don't you?"

Tucker knew he was right. But he didn't want to admit it. He didn't want to know what was too far below the covers. He just wanted to do his job.

"And as for who hires whom, doesn't this happen all over the world? You think we live in some perfect world where only the good guys win? You know that's not true. I guess that's the advantage of living in Europe. We can't save everyone. So we don't even try."

CHAPTER 8

B RANDY HAD CHRISTY take her, Dorie and little Jessica over to the house they were buying. Dorie loved it. Jessica tried several times to escape, heading straight for the narrow stairs.

Dorie's pregnancy was really starting to show, even though she was only five months along. But her body was skin and bones, and the dark circles under her eyes were worrisome. Even Christy noticed and asked Brandy about it while Dorie went out to the car to change Jessica.

"Everything okay at home?" she asked.

"He's waiting on the Navy to get his paperwork processed. At this rate, she said the re-assignment might come just as he is finishing his twentieth year. She's worried the discharge gets processed before his new job comes through."

"That's the Navy for you," signed Christy. "But with so many on Brawley's side, they'd get it fixed. But

I get it. He wants to feel useful."

"Now that he's on outpatient, he has a lot of free time. Unsupervised free time. I just wish he'd help out with Jessica a bit more. I try, but you know."

Christy gave her a hug. "You're a good friend. I'm sure his doctor has explained that he might not be able to be there emotionally for her, to know what to do or how to help her. He's disabled and not himself."

"She knows it, but she's tired, Christy. And they're having twins."

"Yes, well, you let me take some of the burden off your hands. Don't try to help her out alone. Let me get some of the wives and we'll see if we can be more present. You'll see. We stand up for each other, Brandy."

Brandy's heart was beating full of gratitude when Dorie returned to the kitchen area, chasing Jessica.

"Well, that makes six for today. Honestly, she's got the same appetite as her father," said Dorie breathlessly.

"Well then, seems only fair to make him do the cooking, then. If you're supposed to do the changing, I'd say that's a fair tradeoff," laughed Christy.

Jessica had turned several knobs in the kitchen, and they smelled gas. Christy was quick to turn them back to off. Jessica was on to pulling open the drawers and slamming them shut.

Dorie raised her shoulders. "Christy, you re-thinking about having Jess come over to play with your two? You'd better put a helmet on them."

"No, that only happens when we have little Ali and Griffin come over. Our rules are that Ali's slingshot has to be checked at the door like any other weapon."

Dorie touched her belly. "Oh, I just felt one of them move again. Wow."

Brandy knew she'd been concerned about not feeling movement, even though her ultrasounds had been normal and she was reassured the babies were kicking. She hoped that would give her some relief.

"Let me see," Brandy said, placing her palm against Dorie's belly. She felt a slight movement like someone had moved an elbow or heel against the insides of her stomach. "I feel it too! That's cool!"

Christy had taken Jessica outside to the backyard, holding her hand. With the gentle guidance, Jessica walked calmly beside her, her arm outstretched, chattering partial words as she pointed out grass and flowers and followed the motion of a bird.

Dorie turned. "I think you and Tucker are going to be really happy here. What a great neighborhood. You're surrounded by much bigger homes."

"I know it's the right thing to do. Maybe eventually make this a separate unit up top. Give us a little income."

"Good idea. If not, what a great room to paint in."

"I know. Already got the paint!"

When they headed out to the yard, Christy was on the phone but still holding Jessica's hand. Dorie quickly took over.

Christy hung up and then addressed Brandy. "Can you come in to see my loan guy tomorrow morning? He wants to take the application and run the credit."

"Sure."

The three women took turns holding or walking with Jessica as they got to the beach, until she fell asleep in Brandy's arms.

"Today was a good day," said Dorie.

"By now, the guys are probably having coffee and waking up, if any of them slept," added Christy.

Sandpipers escaped from the fast-moving surf as they foraged for sand crabs and other little burrowing creatures. The western sky was turning bright pink.

"Never gets old, does it?" asked Brandy. She rocked from side to side and then took a seat on a large log that was stuck in the sand. Jessica repositioned herself.

"Looks like she's completely out," whispered Dorie.

Brandy gave her a thumbs-up.

Christy surveyed the empty beach and the pink glow of the horizon. "When my mom moved here, this was the first thing she showed me. She'd bought one of those apartments at the Millennium complex. One of the first owners. She loved it here."

Brandy agreed. There was something magic about this place.

THE NEXT MORNING, after filling out the paperwork for her home loan, Brandy called her Dad and invited herself to their house for a quick lunch. She was anxious to hear from Tucker, so spending time with her father and Jillian, his fiancé, would keep her worried mind active with other thoughts.

As they sat down, she told them about the house.

"Only a couple blocks from the beach, and everything around it is huge and remodeled. Dad, I think we stole it," she said.

Jillian smiled as she dished up salad. "That's what I thought when we bought this place. And I was right. Even if it's small, hang onto it and use it as a rental. Don't sell it."

"Not planning to," Brandy returned. "Dad, you've got to come see it one of these days."

"Just arrange it. I'm pretty free."

Jillian brought up the topic Brandy had been avoiding. "When do you hear from Tucker?"

"Actually, we're expecting a call anytime now. Everyone's on pins and needles," she answered.

"Where are they going this time?" her dad asked.

"Not sure," Brandy lied. "But we're not supposed to

talk about it, either. All I know is that they are going back to get someone they didn't get before."

"You mean like a bad guy?" her dad asked.

"You know I can't talk about that. Honestly, we've been through this, Dad."

"Steven, stop that. You know the rules."

Her dad patted her hand. "Sorry, kid."

"You been to the doctor since we saw you last?" Jillian asked.

"Tucker and I saw the baby's heartbeat last week. It was so cute to see such a big guy cry. Kind of touched the little technician, too."

They ran out of things to talk about if they were going to avoid talking about Tucker being gone. She promised she'd arrange a time so they could inspect the house.

ON THE WAY home, she got the call she'd been waiting for.

"Hey there sweetheart. We're here, safe and sound."

"That's great. How was the flight over?"

"Private first-class jet charter. I recommend it highly," Tucker said. "Of course, it would probably mean we couldn't buy that house."

"I'm glad. But I'd rather have the house than the ride."

"Probably the only time in my life I'll get to fly that way. Sat next to the Norwegian Special Forces guy, Sven, remember?"

"Yes. I'm glad he's going with you."

"We are too. So how was your day?" he asked.

"I took Dorie over to the house yesterday. Jessica was a handful, but between the three of us—"

"Three of you?"

"Christy was there too."

"Right. I forgot."

"Anyway, she fell asleep on me as we were walking down the beach. Then this morning, I had lunch with Dad and Jillian and told them all about the house. Tucker, I'm even more convinced it's the right place. It's just magic."

Tucker was quiet, more than she expected. He presented a big yawn and apologized.

"You probably didn't get any rest on the way over, did you?"

"Nope. Sven and I got to talking about stuff. So, honey, if you don't mind, I'm going to sign off and hit the sack."

"No problem, Tucker. Great to hear your voice."

"I'll try to check in again tomorrow, if I can. But there's a chance we'll be dark for a couple of days, so don't worry, okay? Just not sure what the schedule is."

"No worries. Now get some rest. Think I'll turn in

early too. I hope Kyle gives you the day to catch up."

"Oh, forgot to ask, anything about the house I need to know?"

"Not yet. Inspections are in about a week. We might have to make some decisions after we get the reports. I filled out the loan papers this morning, and the broker doesn't think there will be much problem."

"I still can't tell anyone here what we're paying for it," Tucker whispered.

"It's none of their business anyway."

"Okay, well, it's in your capable hands. I'm exercising for all the work you're gonna make me do when we own it." He yawned again. "Hey, I'm gonna have to cut out, or I'll fall asleep here on the phone."

"You go. Get some rest. I'll talk to you tomorrow or whenever. Thanks so much for calling, Tucker. It means a lot to me."

"Nite, sweetheart."

Brandy pulled up to her house, parked the car, and headed to her front door. There was a small package left on the landing step addressed to Tucker. Someone had written on the outside of the box "Baby Gift."

Bringing it inside, she sat on the living room couch and tore open the paper. Inside was a shoebox. When she opened the lid, she found a doll dressed in a sleeper. It wasn't the type of doll she'd ever seen anywhere for sale in the large local stores, and she was surprised by the fact that it wasn't really babyproof, either. Plus, it looked slightly used. She scrounged around the packing paper for a card but found none.

She pulled the doll out of the packing and held it up. The eyes opened and closed when she lay it down and stood it up. She spread the doll's legs so that it would sit on the coffee table in front of her. She went to straighten the arms up into a searching position, like she wanted to be picked up.

But one of the hands on the doll was sliced off.

CHAPTER 9

TUCKER NEVER LIKED sleeping during daylight hours, but he was used to forcing himself. He finally gave up two hours later.

The Team had been housed in a large home not too far from the compound they were going to invade this evening. In fact, Kyle had insisted they drive by it early this morning when they landed.

The lush island was a favorite for Brit vacationers but wasn't as well traveled by American tourists. Parts of it felt like the Caribbean, and other parts, like the crumbling older parts of the city, looked Portuguese or Spanish with the red tiled roofs and stone fencing. He recognized the Spanish Civil Guard uniforms, all well-armed and very visible.

But on top of the hill, where the blue water of the Atlantic contrasted with huge puffy white clouds and overgrown vines with tons of flowers in bright shades of fuscia and coral, it wouldn't take much of a stretch to understand why—for some—it was paradise.

Several of the team had doubled up, but Tucker got a bedroom to himself. Instructions went out that all cell phones were to be turned off and there would be no calls home until after the raid. Kyle told them to try to get a little sleep, and then they'd have a meeting to go over the plan.

He asked Kyle for a moment of his time and was asked to wait. He was waiting for an update from Spec Ops.

The conversation on the flight over with Sven bothered him greatly. He knew he had to inform Kyle, and he was glad Sven didn't make him swear he wouldn't, so that was what he was going to do first chance he got. He couldn't stand the thought of bringing his brothers into a situation they weren't one hundred percent up-to-date on. That was always the problem, getting accurate intel. The relationship of the Special Agent to the victim and her father was something his team should know about.

Now he had second thoughts about Sven. Perhaps he'd been played. Though he liked the guy, perhaps he wasn't the dude Tucker originally thought he was. He was telling the truth when he told Sven he never liked the politics of the job. He was just there to get it done. Politics was a dirty word, as it was for most the team guys. It was just not a factor, even in today's situations.

It muddled the decision-making dangerously. A fighting man got orders. He wasn't supposed to think about the consequences. Likewise, it wasn't fair to make him fight with one hand behind his back or without accurate information. Having to think too much about the consequences gave a tactical disadvantage to the team on a mission.

Tucker tried to lie back again to get some sleep but gave up after a few minutes. He got up, changed his tee shirt, slipped on a pair of pants, and ran downstairs barefoot in search of his LPO.

Special Agent Fielding was still up, having a cup of coffee and studying a topography map. It completely caught him off guard, and before he could retreat back upstairs to find Kyle, she spotted him.

"Morning, Tucker. You can't sleep either?"

He looked for something, anything to focus on other than her young face. He knew she was going to try to extract questions of him, and that's not what he wanted until he talked to Kyle.

"Nah. Your old friend, Sven, kept me up." He poured himself a coffee that had been freshly brewed.

"So I heard." She slowly rose and walked into the kitchen with her mug in hand, extending it for a refill. He obliged, still not making eye contact.

He turned his back on her, looking for some milk or cream in the refrigerator and was happy to find it well-stocked with everything, including chilled wine, beers, fruits and vegetables and milk. There also was a quart of half-and-half, which he grabbed to top off his coffee.

The warm liquid felt like vitamins this morning. He took another long gulp and nearly finished off the mug. She was watching him, not letting go. Now he'd have to deal with her, and he felt ill-prepared.

"Tucker, I—"

"Save it," he barked, which he could see surprised her. "I don't like what Sven told me, and this little act you two are playing is very, very dangerous."

Her eyes filled up with water.

"It's not an act. These are horrible people, Tucker. My only hope for getting Jenna out is your team."

"Tell me how that works. You disable the team you say is your saving grace? Just how are any of these guys, who you've weaponized to be your family's fighting force, to put their lives on the line for someone who doesn't give a damn about giving them the truth? I'm all ears, Kelly."

She sucked in air as if he'd punched her. Here was another example why having a woman on a mission was a bad idea. Tucker grew more furious as he talked to her. She wasn't the hardened, seasoned professional he was used to seeing in combat zones, the CIA operatives he'd seen do interrogations. Those ladies were tough and mostly well-respected. It was obvious she had no military training like the CIA gals did. Even the language specialists could defend themselves and had lots of marksmanship and combat training.

This lady looked like she read Cosmo and had her nails done regularly.

"I get it. What I was about to say was I wanted to tell Kyle. And I think we should, this morning first thing."

"You think?" Tucker spit back. He poured another cup of coffee and added more cream.

She followed him to the living room but they both remained standing. He glanced around him to make sure no one else was up to overhear their conversation.

"What's this thing with Sven?" he asked.

"You jealous?"

Tucker nearly threw his coffee at her. His blood boiled. He inhaled, closed his eyes and waited for the anger to fade away.

"That was cruel of me. I'm sorry."

"Your attitude sucks, lady. You think this is some kind of game? How the hell did you get your little ass on this mission? Now we have to protect you, as well as get your clueless sister-in-law."

Kelly sat down and focused on her knees. After a few tense moments, she murmured, "You're right."

Tucker wasn't a complete asshole, and he realized

perhaps she'd been drawn in with the best of intentions, but it was a plan created by a non-combat type individual, and it was a very bad idea.

"Jenna lacks common sense. She ran off to Africa without her father's permission. She's never been smart. If she survives, life will change for her."

"But she has a father with billions to waste on operations he thinks he can plan. This kind of world, this arena is not one you can do this in. This isn't a corporate takeover or some boardroom proxy war. These are big-time major drug and human trafficking, cartels. Heads of governments are all in on it, even the police or armed forces. What I've seen over in Nigeria and what I've been told is horrible. You have no idea how those people live. You can't just go in there and be a 'nice person.' These people—" He stopped because he could see his point had already been made. Kelly was nodding her head.

"I get it."

"So Sven. What's up with that? I need to know."

"He's the one who found Dad. Sorry, I call Mr. Riley dad. I know that's offensive to you."

"Oh, cut the crap, Kelly."

"When he contacted him, that's when Mr. Riley told him about me." Kelly looked up at Tucker, and, although he was still boiling with anger, he did feel sorry for her. Just a smidge.

"Go on."

"He agreed to bankroll an operation on the condition that I was to remain part of the team and was to be protected."

"And?"

"And because of my language training."

"But you don't know anything about these people."

"But I do. My husband—he got involved with some guys I thought were just locals. He used drugs recreationally. I was just getting started with my State Department final phase. I was worried I'd not pass a background check. I moved to Washington D.C. to complete my training, and we separated for a short time. That's when he overdosed. I was devastated, and I thought it would end my position. Turns out, they knew all along."

"Geez. Who the hell is running things, anyway?"

"We agreed to go forward, and I reverted back to my maiden name so there wouldn't be any taint. I'd study the drug and human trafficking businesses, and eventually help them identify the bad actors. I was to provide background and research for our diplomats who were risking their lives to try to work out arrangements with leaders in foreign countries, specifically African countries. And I'm still motivated to do that. I feel I owe it to Jack."

Tucker sat across from Kelly. The wheels were

turning. Tucker found her convincing, but he knew this information had to get to Kyle without delay. "Do you think Jack was targeted at all?"

"You mean, because of his dad?"

"Exactly."

"I wondered about that, but I have no real way of knowing for sure. That's always been a question Sven's had too. He asked it in the briefing, remember?"

"Yup, I do."

"Jack's father was always a heavy anti-drug guy. He's contributed to many organizations to combat opioid abuse in the Northwest. I think Jack was a bit naive about what he could handle. He always wanted his dad to set him up in a business he could run, but Mr. Riley was lavish with the donations and stingy when it came to his kids. They'd had a falling out. Who knows who knew what was going on there? He went downhill fast, after I left."

Tucker thought about his own parents in Oregon, who had attempted to run a medical marijuana business, a grow farm, and decided to give it up because of the inherent dangers. He was never so relieved when he found out his dad went back to work as a mechanic. But they still had the land.

"Kelly, I think it's beyond time we need to get this information to Kyle." He leaned forward, placing his elbows on his knees. "It's his call. He might want to abort."

"I understand."

"Tell me about Sven. You trust him?"

"With my life. He's solid. I didn't even know about what you guys did. I think he wants them as badly as I do. He sees this as an opportunity to make a difference. Honest."

Tucker still didn't like it, but he knew exactly what he had to do next.

CHAPTER 10

"STAY RIGHT WHERE you are, Brandy. I'll be over in five minutes." Brawley's voice was low, nearly a whisper, and she could tell he was trying to hide their conversation from Dorie.

Brandy checked her phone and still hadn't received a message from Tucker. Instinct made her lock all her windows. She didn't know the significance of the doll, but the fact that it had been addressed to Tucker and had been designated "baby gift" led her to suspect there was some history involving the last mission, and Brawley would know about it. She still trusted him enough to believe he'd understand what next to do.

True to his word, Brawley steamed into the driveway and burst through the front door as soon as she unlocked it without saying a word. He stared down at the doll on the table, instantly used the box to scoop it up, and then threw it out the back door—as far away from the house as he could. He waited. Nothing further happened.

"What's going on?" she asked, standing beside him.

"Pack. You have to get out of this house right now, Brandy. I'm going to take you over to our place, and then we'll figure out where we'll go."

"We? What do you mean we?"

"I don't have time to explain it, but get your clothes packed right now. Take anything you care about but quickly."

She ran to the bedroom, pulled out a suitcase and started throwing things in. It struck her as she was putting underwear and tops into the bag she didn't know what kind of trip she was packing for.

Brawley had removed the carpet in their closet, accessed Tucker's gun stash, and started loading up things he hadn't taken with him on the deployment.

"Why are you doing that?"

"So no one else will find them."

"Who are we talking about?"

"Just pack, dammit."

Brandy was instantly in tears, confused, afraid, and heaving for breath. Brawley ran to her side, gave her a hug like he'd never done before, and whispered, "We have a problem here. You have to remain calm. I'm here to get you out of this house ASAP and to someplace safe. I promise I'll explain everything when we get there."

She managed to nod her head against his chest and untangle herself from his grip. She felt the cold realization that the dream world she was living in had been shattered by the real world. Something was out there trying to take it all away. She wasn't going to second-guess it. She'd just act. That's what Tucker would do.

"Birth records, marriage certificates, your passport, bank records? You have them in one place?" Brawley asked.

"Yes, in the box in the pantry. Everything's in there. I have a file drawer for paid bills—"

"Leave them. I'll get your box. Do a double check and make sure nothing too personal, too important is left behind."

He tossed the extra duty bag over his shoulder on his way to the pantry. Brandy stood in the middle of the bedroom, searching, then started going through drawers. She found a filled journal of Tucker's and decided that should come with her. She scanned the bed, her eyes filling with tears again. Bending down, she lovingly straightened the covers and plumped the pillows, as if it would be the last time she would touch that place that had brought her and Tucker so much delight. If Brawley wasn't with her, she'd just curl up into a ball and stay there under the covers, where it was warm and where it smelled like the man she missed so much now.

Now Brandy understood how people felt when they had to pack for a natural disaster and hoped she hadn't left anything behind.

Brawley grabbed her suitcase as she locked the front door. "Everything's locked, even all the windows," she said hurriedly.

"Good." Brawley tossed her suitcase into the back seat of his truck as she climbed into the cab.

He checked both directions on the street before he pulled out. Brandy didn't see anything out of the ordinary. There were several vacant cars and small trucks parked along the curb, and one turning into a driveway. It was nearly dark, and most of the families living there would be having dinner, she thought.

He raced down the street and headed for the freeway, checking his rearview mirror constantly.

"Where are we going?"

"I'm just going to make sure." Then he dialed someone, still checking the mirrors. He mumbled to himself, "Come on. Come on, pick up."

They entered the freeway, which was clogged with late commuter traffic, causing them to slow down. Brandy heard squawking on the other end of the phone. Brawley began leaving a message.

"Collins. Hey, we got a situation here. I'm with Brandy. I'm taking her over to my place. I gotta talk to you, man. Like pronto."

Brandy had met this mysterious Collins man at one of the graduations. He was their team handler, the go-to guy in case they needed anything done for them by the Navy or to help locate an asset.

Brawley finally relaxed as they weaved in and around slower traffic until they passed two exits. At the third exit, he veered off and doubled back toward the direction of his house, using smaller streets that threaded along the freeway. He turned to her, asking, "So, you tried calling Tucker, right?"

"Of course. I called him first." She knew he didn't want questions, but she didn't care. "What is it with that doll? What's going on, Brawley, or what do you think is going on?"

"I'm not sure. And I can't explain much, but that doll was very clearly a warning. Like a night letter."

"What?"

"Over in Iraq and Afghanistan, the bad guys would leave notes on the doors of some of the people they were targeting, or on a school door, warning the kids and women to stay away."

"Because?"

"Because, in many cases, that house, that school was targeted for an attack. Not always, but the night letters put the fear of God into the villagers. It was very effective that way."

Brandy sat still and swallowed hard, staring out the

windshield of Brawley's truck, her stomach churning. Why would anyone target her, or her house, or Tucker? She felt the heavy thumping of her heart, and the way her mouth was parched. She knew she had to calm down, for the sake of the baby she was carrying.

"But that's over *there*. This is *here*. This is the US," she dared to whisper, knowing Brawley wouldn't like her question.

Brawley shrugged, checked his surroundings again, and then began to slow down. He exhaled then repositioned his hands on the steering wheel. "I don't mean to scare you, but a lot of the team guys have thought for some time that the enemy is trying to bring the war to us. At least to show us that they can. With all of our border issues, San Diego would be an easy place to infiltrate, get in the country, and conduct mayhem. They won't win, Brandy. They'll never win, but they want us to know they're coming. They want to invoke fear. That's what that doll is about."

"But what's the significance of it—of that missing hand?"

"I can't really talk about it until I have permission, but I promise you, I'll do it just as soon as I can. You'll just have to hang on a bit. Can you do that for me?"

Brandy nodded.

"And I need you to keep Dorie calm too. That's a tall order, but I have to focus on something else first, and I've got a couple other calls to make. I need her to remain calm until we figure out the next step."

"But—"

"Please, Brandy. I can't give you any more than that, but I need your help. It's that important. Tucker would do the same thing if it was reversed. You gotta trust me."

Brandy was suddenly felt grateful, no matter what Brawley had been through, that he was with her and not with the rest of the team overseas. She never thought she'd feel that way about his breakdown, but right now, she could see that all his training had kicked in and he was totally focused, thinking clearly, and was someone she could count on.

And that's exactly what she intended to do.

When they arrived at the Hanks' home, Dorie had set the dinner preparation aside and was reading a story to Jessica. Her eyes got huge when she saw Brandy enter the room right behind her husband.

"When you said you had to go pick up something, well, I didn't expect this, Brawley."

"Hey Dorie," Brandy said as she wheeled her suitcase through the front door, then bent and gave her a kiss on her cheek, giving another one to Jessica.

"Dada!" The little one outstretched her arms, and Brawley picked her up. While Jessica was playing with Brawley's beard, her dad tried to explain the situation to his wife.

"Brandy got a package delivered to their house. It was a warning that she's not safe. I brought her over here, but Dorie, honey, we got to pack up too. If they know where she lives, they're going to know where we do too."

"Oh my God! No!" Dorie stammered as she stood, her hand over her mouth. "This can't be happening."

Brandy threw her arms around her to calm her down. "We hope not, but Brawley's just trying to be careful. Apparently, you may be in danger here. You need to get things put together just like I did. He's trying to find out what's going on. Even if it turns out to be a false alarm, we have to plan to get someplace safe for now. Help me, okay?"

"Is Tucker okay?"

"They've gone dark. No word from him yet, so he doesn't know," said Brandy.

"As far as we know," inserted Brawley. "Let's get some clothes packed for all three of us. I'll get some other things we might need, and then I'd like to be out of here in like ten minutes. Can we do that?"

Dorie nodded, walking like a zombie to their bedroom. Brawley handed Jessica to Brandy when his cell rang.

"Thank God, Collins." After a brief acknowledgement, Brawley continued, "A package was delivered to

Tucker's house, and Brandy picked it up. It was a doll wrapped in paper. Labeled as a baby gift."

He paused for Collin's comment.

"No, she opened it. And yes, I'll tell her. When she called me, I raced over and tossed the thing in the backyard. It's still there now, the paper it was wrapped in, the box. Everything. Someone needs to go check it out. I didn't see any wires, powder, or anything suspicious, but who knows? You need to get the bomb squad."

Brandy tried to get Jessica interested in the book but wasn't having much luck. She saw Brawley remind Dorie to pack certain things while he was on the phone with Collins.

"Listen, sir, the right hand was cut off the doll. It wasn't a new toy, but rather like something from a used toy store or charity store. And in light of what went on in Nigeria with the doctor, I just know these assholes are somehow here. Can that even be possible?"

Brawley listened to some further instructions and then hung up.

"Okay, we're to get to a motel nearby until we get more details. I'm going to call Christy right now. Let's complete the packing and take off, okay?"

Both Dorie and Brandy nodded. Even Jessica did so.

"He told me to pack banking information, passports or marriage licenses, anything legal, personal, too," Brandy reminded her best friend in a whisper.

Dorie stood before her in tears. "This doesn't make any sense."

"But thank God we have Brawley."

Dorie went back to her search while Brandy walked Jessica to the living room again. She overheard Brawley on the phone with Christy Lansdowne.

"—No, absolutely not, Christy. I'm not going to put you or your family in danger. Collins instructed me to get a couple of rooms at the Marriott. But if Kyle calls, be sure to tell him to contact Collins. He's arranging a team to go over to the house, and then they'll come here and do a quick search. Do not open the door for anybody. No parcels, got it? And he'll want you to alert the other wives when the time comes, so be ready, okay?"

When Brawley hung up, she asked him again about the package. "You told Collins you'd tell me something. What's that?"

"That wasn't your fault, but if you ever get something like that mailed or delivered and you don't recognize who it's from, you don't open it. You call someone who will get in touch with Naval Security."

She must have been shaking because Jessica was touching her cheeks, looking for tears.

"Brandy, a lot of these rules are changing. It didn't

used to be this way. Same reasons we want you off social media, not posting anything on Facebook. The bad guys are out there, and unfortunately, the families are targets."

Jessica was squirming in her arms, so Brawley took her. "Let's get this show on the road." He called to Dorie. "Are you ready?"

"The passports. I forgot where I put them," she answered.

"I got 'em in my duty bag. All set?"

"I know I'm forgetting something, but I can't even think right now." Dorie passed him and headed to the kitchen. "Let me just clean up these dinner things, and—"

But Brawley was right behind her, gently taking a pan from her hands and speaking to her softly, "Sweetheart, leave it. We gotta go. No one cares about that right now. We gotta get out of here."

As they ran to the truck and placed the bags inside, Brandy slipped her phone out from her purse and noted there still was no answer from Tucker.

She wasn't even sure what to tell him.

CHAPTER 11

KYLE WAS STUDYING diagrams and maps when Tucker entered his room.

"Kyle, I think we have a problem," he said.

His LPO looked up, gave him a frown, and then went back to looking over a floorplan, probably of the house they were to invade tonight.

"What's got you bothered?" his Chief mumbled.

"There's something you don't know about Sven and Kelly."

That got Kyle's attention. "Oh yeah?"

"First of all, Sven and Kelly spent time together gathering all the surveillance on the Dutch guy's house."

"I know that. So?"

"But you don't know that Kelly is Jenna's sister-in-law."

Kyle was cool about it, pretending to get occupied with the maps. Then with one sweep of his arm, he wiped everything off his bed. "Fuck me."

"Exactly."

"How did you hear this?"

"Sven told me on the ride over. Kelly was married to Jenna's brother, who was our benefactor's son."

"*Was?*"

"As in he died of an overdose."

"I get it now. It would have been nice if someone had told me. So what you're saying is all this help we're getting is partly personal—well, that part we knew, but we didn't know members of this team had a personal stake in the outcome as well. I fucking don't like this."

"What are we going to do?"

"A little late for that, don't you think? Unless you don't feel you can trust her or Sven?"

"That's a tough one. I just don't trust anyone who isn't honest right out of the box, Kyle. That's not how we roll."

"Yeah, but it's what we get sometimes, right?"

Tucker chuckled darkly. "It's not the first and won't be the last we get faulty intel. Story of our job, right, Kyle?"

"Amen to that."

"So, what's next?"

Kyle stood up. He stretched his arms above his head and behind his neck then rolled down as if to touch his nose to his knees in a yoga stretch. He let out a big exhale and grumbled, "We come to Jesus."

TUCKER'S JOB WAS to get everyone assembled in the great room off the kitchen. Not many were happy about this. Sven nodded respectfully toward him, standing in the shadows at the corner of the room. Kelly was making another pot of coffee.

"Okay, guys," Kyle began. "We've just been updated on some information on this mission I want you in on. Sven and Kelly have a little secret, it turns out. And let me say, for the record, if one of you guys ever does anything like this to me, I promise I'll get you busted, and off the teams. I'll make sure you spend the rest of your miserable Naval careers peeling potatoes on a sub."

"What the hell?" Fredo remarked. "What happened?"

"No, man. What you doin' fuckin' with our LPO?" grumbled T.J., looking around the room. Several others, including Jake, Armando, and Jameson agreed.

DeWayne Huggles pointed to Kelly. "I never liked you!" Tucker could see all his earlier concerns had come crashing back to haunt him. Haunt them all.

"So which one of you wants to tell the team?" barked Kyle.

"I'll do it." Sven stepped from the corner and studied all their faces before he began. "I got a tip that the

American nurse was being held here on the island. I did some digging into her family background, because I was getting nothing from the Africa Corp folks. I was on hold, and, well, I got tired of waiting. I knew time was of the essence and they were dealing with something much bigger than they were capable of handling. And the big problem is that they don't pay ransoms, not because they don't value their people, but they never have enough money."

Tucker watched the faces of the men remain hard. So far, Sven hadn't cracked their veneer.

"I discovered who Jenna's father was. He's a very wealthy investor, did well in the tech industry in the Pacific Northwest, and was semi-retired, donating his vast fortune to worthy causes. The man's a good guy."

Sven cocked his head and looked across the room at Kelly, who didn't return his gaze. "I contacted him and told him I thought I could lead a team to rescue her. He didn't know me from Adam, and I'm sure he didn't trust me, either, so I flew out to Oregon and had a sit down. And he introduced me to Kelly, who happens—and this is the part you guys didn't know until now—to be his daughter-in-law. Kelly was married to Jenna's brother, the old man's son."

The swearing would have been stronger if there hadn't been a lady present, even though Kelly was part of the source of irritation.

Kelly interrupted Sven's story. "Jack died nearly two years ago while I was finishing my State Department specialty training. Prior to that, Jack and I had worked lower level jobs in Africa together for State and other departments. It's how we met. Jenna heard the stories and always wanted to go there. My qualifications still stand and are true. But you didn't know that Jenna is related to me by marriage. And I feel very responsible for her capture and demise. My father-in-law is a very rich and powerful man who wants to save the only child he has left."

"We have a say here, Chief?" asked Coop.

"You can try. I'm not sure what good it does," answered Kyle.

"We're kind of fucked," whispered Armando.

"But I will say this. If any of you want to abort, I'm not going to stand in your way. I owe it to you, though the Navy would think otherwise. You were brought here under false pretenses, and I didn't want you to think I did it. You gotta trust me. But most important is the question of do you trust these two?" Kyle added, pointing to Sven and Kelly.

"What about the Headshed?" Tyler asked.

Kyle stood up and rubbed the back of his neck with his hand. "Well, I received the go, and told them we're going silent for twenty-four hours. I could just not call them. They're not expecting to hear from me until tomorrow morning, and with good news, too. We have no backup, so nothing had to be coordinated."

Tucker and everyone in the room knew it was a career-ending decision.

"Not fair you taking that risk, Kyle. I don't like it," said Coop.

Armando agreed. "Something goes wrong, maybe we all get tossed, but this will come down on you hardest. I don't like it either, Kyle."

Kyle smiled back at two of his oldest friends on the team. "Then we don't screw up."

That generated another level of swearing in several languages. Over the next few minutes, everyone had their say. Some spoke to themselves. Some spoke to the person sitting next to them or to the room. But by the end of the few minutes, the decision had been made, and everyone was on board as a team. This was how the boardroom of a spec ops team functioned.

The mission remained a go.

Sven and Kelly took over the discussion, showing floorplans of the house and the position of the posted guards and what kinds of firepower they were carrying. They detailed the security cameras and electric perimeter fencing.

The good news was that even though the Dutch billionaire had spent a lot of money on security, there were huge gaps in his coverage and safety precautions.

The bulk of his protection was his reliance on the men he hired. Tucker knew that any one SEAL on the team was worth at least twenty of them, so the odds outweighed the bad guys significantly.

Tucker asked another question of Kelly. "What kind of mindset will she be in? Did you see her or observe her condition at all?"

Kelly took a deep inhale. "Yes, she's being chained to a bedframe in the bedroom. She doesn't have the freedom to roam the house. She gets to shower, use the bathroom, but she doesn't go anywhere outside the bedroom. And,"—Kelly's breath hitched—"he beats her. I think he's given her drugs too. Other than the obvious sexual abuse, which must be horrible, I think she's physically fine. But the sex, judging from how she looks, is nowhere near consensual."

Several of the team guys swore. People who abused women were always at the top of their kill list.

"We both thought, based on how Mr. VanValle was acting, he was going to tire of her very soon. She's a mess, really. We need to tell it like it is, Kelly."

"Of course," she whispered back.

"But she's strong enough? I mean, she can walk, run on her own?" asked Coop.

Kelly and Sven nodded.

"Part of the reason I didn't want you to abort this mission is, well, I don't think she has much time left.

She has no value to him." Sven again surveyed the room. It generated lots of head nodding. Her life expectancy was short. They all understood this.

Kyle re-traced what their positions would be. He ordered his snipers, Armando and Jameson, to find a good vantage point to cover the front door and the vehicles. Fredo would pass out Invisios. The whole team was ordered to carry everything they brought, since there might not be the chance to come back to the villa. Kyle showed them the best escape route by road and a secondary road, if they had to hike out, where they could get somewhere and commandeer a vehicle, if necessary.

"We got about five hours until it's dark. I recommend everyone do a power rest. Change your clothes, re-pack your bags, and check your equipment." Kyle's command was well heeded.

Kyle divided the men into two groups for transport to the Dutchman's house and then hopefully beyond. Their villa came with a ten-passenger Opel van, and a larger Jeep SUV, so there would be plenty of room. Sven volunteered to load up the vehicles with waters and things from the house they might need during the stakeout while everyone else rested and prepared.

Tucker went upstairs, set his alarm and was going to take a quick nap. He got out his journal to write a few sentences to Brandy.

Not exactly what I was expecting this time around, but then I'm supposed to handle anything that's thrown at me. Good news is I doubt we'll be here longer than an overnight and that makes me real happy.

I hate sleeping during daylight hours, but I'll be working at night, so that's just how it goes.

Learned some things about family dynamics I don't ever want to see in our family. It's like there's us and then the rest of the planet. We're here to fix a mistake we didn't make. That's always the job, though. If we're lucky, we'll be able to get information on the operation we're fighting so the next group can go further with the cleanup.

The islands are a mixture of cultures, not unlike Africa. But this place is part of Spain, and though it's close, it doesn't feel like Africa at all. The buildings are colorful, like the Caribbean, but they use more rock and stone, and many of their streets are cobblestone. Lots of churches tolling all day long. It seems a little more prosperous and not as many inhabitants.

We're up high where it's cooler, and if I concentrate, I can smell the saltwater way down below. Where we're staying, the homes are for wealthy world travelers or vacation rentals for the jet-setting crowd. We have two nearly new vans, more bathrooms than bedrooms, and a refrigerator the guys are going to regret they won't even begin to tackle.

I miss Brawley. Doesn't seem like a mission without him. My thoughts are with all of you. Tell my son (I know you think it's a girl, but I don't) to be nice to his mama and to let you sleep. Hope Jessica is behaving. I owe you all a nice, long walk on the beach when I get home. That's what I'm going to think about while I turn in for a bit.

Then it's showtime.

Love you more each day, Brandy.

Right on time, Tucker was awakened and was ready to go in minutes. He double-checked his bedroom and bath for anything he'd forgotten.

Downstairs, the group stocked up on food from the refrigerator. There were energy drinks on the counter, along with granola bars and peanuts. Tucker grabbed what he could, stashing things here and there in the pockets he'd fashioned.

He piled into the Opel with Kyle, Armando, and several others. Sven and Kelly rode in the Jeep with Jake, Tyler, and DeWayne.

They passed the house as they had coming up the twisting road, driving farther down to a wide driveway with a metal electric fence from a neighboring house behind the shoulder. They listened for traffic and heard none. Quietly, they grabbed their duty bags and exited the vehicles, staying to the sides of the road in the shadows. As they approached the compound, Armando and Jameson split off to position themselves on two carport rooftops that would give perfect vantage.

The rest of the team advanced, splitting up into groups as planned. Kelly and DeWayne were to get closest to the house to listen and check on Jenna's condition, so Tucker and Kyle helped her up into a tree that hovered over the wall so she could climb down. Huggles followed behind.

They split up into two groups on either side of the large gate entrance. Two guards smoked cigarettes and engaged in whispered small talk. Silently, the two groups scaled the outer walls, carefully cutting the razor wire installed at the top, and dropped into the compound yard. A dog barked, which made them freeze. Coop threw a small rock in the opposite direction, away from the house, which distracted the dog. They heard voices coming to check, two flashlights sending beams through the cactus and other exotic plants in the yard. Tucker's group lay flat on the ground until the lights were turned off and the dog lost interest.

The tiny squawk in Tucker's ear told him Armando

and Jameson were in place. Kelly whispered she had a visual on Jenna, who was sleeping. Alone.

Huggles confirmed the location of the Dutchman in the house, watching TV in the living room. "He's got a big dog with him, dammit," Huggles whispered.

"I got Dutchie. Jameson's got the dog," Armando confirmed over the Invisio.

Kyle gave the instructions. "On three, two, one."

Tucker quickly disabled one of the sentries, while T.J. did the other, tossing their semi-automatics into the bushes. Two high-pitched bursts tore through the night as the man with the flashlight fell next to the patrol dog, who had also been hit.

"Sentries secure," said T.J.

Tucker heard several other comments, and then Kyle gave the perimeter secure call.

They were expecting an additional four men on the inside, but Tucker could only count two. DeWayne responded that two bodies were sleeping in a bedroom off the back.

"And Jenna?" asked Kyle.

"Still asleep. She's alone," answered Kelly.

Cooper indicated he'd dismantled the sliding glass door lock on her bedroom. Fredo had picked the front door.

Again, the count from Kyle, "Three, two, one, go!"

The whine from Armando and Jameson's long

guns was followed by the tinkling of a glass window being breached. It gave VanValle just enough time to look up as his forehead exploded. Simultaneously, the dog, sleeping down at his feet, was hit without waking up. The team entered the house from all sides. Tyler and Coop disabled the two sleeping men. The two who sat at the dining room table stood with their hands up when they saw their employer and the dog die in a burst of red spray. Their wrists and ankles were secured, and their heads were covered with two bloodied pillowcases from their teammate's bedroom.

Kyle's team had managed to breach the house then disable or kill everyone without a single shout out or sound of a weapon firing. All Tucker could hear as various rooms in the home were declared clear was the whimpering coming from the back bedroom. Jenna was sobbing uncontrollably. As Tucker approached, he saw Kelly take out a pair of jeans and sweatshirt and tennis shoes and hurriedly got her dressed.

Jenna's lip was split and she had a black eye. It made him want to throw up.

Kyle instructed them to look for cell phones, any laptops they could take. Six were found and zippered into duty bags. On the table were some papers, and all of them were confiscated. Pictures of the bodies were taken, including the two dogs that unfortunately had to be sacrificed. Kyle gave the message for the shooters to come in with the all clear.

Just as quietly as they arrived, the team left, this time using the main gate entrance. They left the TV on, as well as all the house lights. They ran back down the road by starlight to their vehicles and waited for Armando and Jameson to catch up. Then they were on their way.

The whole operation had taken no more than ten minutes. With any luck, they'd be at the airport in three hours and back on that nice jet, perhaps drinking champagne, before daylight.

Tucker monitored himself and discovered his blood pressure hadn't risen more than a few clicks. It was just like the old days. The job was done. The only thing he focused on now was getting home.

CHAPTER 12

THE CHEERFUL DESK receptionist inappropriately smiled and asked them how their day was going. Brawley couldn't resist.

"Fucked."

The young brunette fluttered her eyelids several times and then responded with, "I'm sorry to hear that." She clicked a few keystrokes and then regrouped, adding, "Now I'll need your driver's license and one form of payment for incidentals."

Brawley didn't quibble or ask to make sure the Navy was picking up the tab. He just gave the young girl what she wanted.

Still holding the sleeping Jessica, Brandy noted all the places in the lobby where someone could hide and not be detected. She looked for anyone who had more than a passing interest in them and found none.

The smile was still plastered on the desk clerk's face as she directed them to the elevator and asked if they needed help with their luggage. Brandy guessed she received a "special" look from Brawley, because the young girl stepped back from the counter and then just watched as they scampered toward the tower elevator.

Dorie struggled with one suitcase and a duty bag. Brawley had the heavy one with the guns and two others strapped across his chest and could easily outrun them all. Brandy was able to tow her wheeling suitcase without problem, but Jessica was getting very heavy. The elevator dropped them at the fourteenth floor.

Two rooms had been provided, which connected. Brandy lay Jessica down on her bed and instructed Brawley and Dorie to take the other room for privacy.

Brawley made sure Dorie got off her feet. Her skin was pale and a bit clammy.

"She doesn't look too good, Brawley."

"I know it. I think I should get some food. She missed dinner."

"Let me order something. Maybe some soup, a sandwich or something. You want anything?"

He shook his head. "Go ahead. I'm going to see if Collins has anything yet. And I'll tell Christy where we are and let her know we got out without incident."

"You owe me an explanation. You know that, don't you?" Brandy wasn't going to let Brawley off the hook until she was given as many details as he could give.

"Make the room service call. I'll get done with Collins and Christy, and we'll talk."

Several minutes after the food was delivered, Brawley closed the adjoining door behind him and took up a seat at the desk in Brandy's room. Jessica was snoring soundly. The two of them shared some potato wedges and two bowls of hearty soup.

"She didn't want anything, but I left it by her bed. I think she just needed water," he whispered.

"Good." Brandy waited for him to fulfill his promise.

"Last time over, we were to check on groups that do human trafficking and run drugs and guns. We were just there to get information and set up a base camp so we could go back and forth for a bigger operation to be done at a later date. But what happened was that we ran into a small militia group who had already ambushed a team of aid workers trying to give vaccinations and medical treatment to the villagers and several schools. They're international aid workers, partly sponsored by the U.N."

"Okay."

"So our safe house got compromised, and we became a rescue operation. We were able to free three medics and two females, one of whom was a doctor who gave aid to a dying rebel soldier. The kid didn't make it, after she had to do an emergency amputation to try to save his life. They blamed the doctor and cut off her hand."

Brandy's stomach lurched and she had to work to keep its contents down.

"Someone who knows about that mission sent the doll, I'm convinced. Collins thinks so too. They're inspecting it now, but we didn't have any chatter or warning that something like this was being planned. But it clearly is an attack on Tucker, through you."

"Is Tucker safe, then?"

"Well, they're not in Africa now, so I assume so. But now I'm not sure what information they have. If they know you're alone, then they know something."

Brandy checked her phone with no result. "If I could just talk to him."

"Believe me, the SOF Command is trying to get hold of Kyle."

"How did they know where we lived? How could that be? It's not like he wears his uniform everywhere. I mean, does this mean that someone has been following us? Could they be following me?"

Brawley stared back at her, his lips in a straight line, no expression to his eyes. He was masking. She knew it well. Brandy looked away.

"Honestly, some days I feel like we should be housing families on base, for protection, like they do outside the U.S. But these are different times, and the enemy is getting resourceful."

"Has this happened before?"

"Here and there. More like incidents with locals who had some kind of an axe to grind. That's why we ask all the families to be careful. It's also why I never go anywhere unless I'm armed. None of us do."

Brawley's cell rang. "Christy must have gotten my message." He put the phone to his ear. "We're safe. Haven't heard anything yet. How about you?"

He listened. Brandy wasn't able to make out Christy's words.

"I promise you'll be the first to know, Christy. I'd get the kids ready, just in case. Just put a couple days of clothes together if they ask you to leave."

The phone call was brief. Brandy planned to call her later, after she'd had a good night's sleep. Right now, buying a house was just not high on her list of priorities. Keeping everyone that she loved safe was.

JESSICA HAD MIRACULOUSLY slept through the entire night, and it frightened Brandy so much she woke the child up herself. After the little one got her bearings, and realized she wasn't in bed with her mother, she began crying for her. The door between their two rooms was still open, and Dorie stepped through in seconds.

"I'd check the bed. More than likely, you are sleeping in a puddle, Brandy."

"Oh geez," she said as she felt the wet spot nearly a foot in circumference.

"Better get used to it, sweetie," Dorie said in farewell as she exited to the other room, the toddler in her arms.

Brandy left another message for Tucker and then decided to shower and get dressed. Afterward, she joined the other room for the breakfast they'd ordered.

"So there's nothing yet, I take it?" asked Brandy.

"Nada. Collins told me to expect some investigators this morning. Navy Intel."

"I tried calling Tucker again. I didn't leave any detail."

"Are we just to stay here all day? In the motel room?" asked Dorie.

"For now."

"Sure would like to know if my house is okay," she mumbled as she fed Jessica.

"What if they know we came here?" Brandy wondered.

Brawley's cell went off, and Collins told him two officers from NCIS Domestic Terrorism unit were on their way.

The two Special Agents, one an older woman and one a young man looking fresh out of college, presented their cards and both showed their shields. Brawley introduced his wife and Brandy and mentioned that Tucker had been on the mission with him to Nigeria but was overseas now.

"So, Mrs. Hudson," asked the woman, "did you see anyone at your residence earlier in the day? Someone perhaps hanging around the street somewhere, or someone you've not seen before?"

"No. I left in the morning. Came back at night. I wasn't expecting anything, so I really didn't look."

"How about your neighbors?"

"I didn't talk to them. Brawley came over and got me out of there. I didn't have time. Haven't you questioned them?"

"I believe we have, Mrs. Hudson, but was wondering if anyone had said anything about someone checking out your home."

"No. Tucker has a sixth sense about things like this, and he said nothing. I mean, he always checks out a room wherever we go. Just his habit, I guess."

"We didn't find any video surveillance on your front door, Mrs. Hudson, or did we miss it?"

"No, we don't have anything like that."

"What did you find out about the doll?" asked Brawley.

"In a minute, Mr. Hanks." The female agent flipped through a tiny notebook and stopped at a page. "Were you, Mr. Hanks, in any public places recently where you could have been identified as a member of the SEAL community?"

Brawley thought about it but shook his head. "Nothing out of the ordinary. I mean, we go to the Scupper. We don't announce who we are, but we sit together. Everyone kind of knows it's tradition. Tourists and people we don't know are in there all the time, too, but we never really talk to them or make much out of the job. Mostly people just watch, and if they get curious, we leave."

Both the agents nodded. After a series of further questions, the female, more senior of the two, began to reveal small portions of the investigation. "The doll is loaded with prints. Must be fifty or more. Nothing came up that we have a record of. We found carpet and clothing fibers, spilled juice and food. It's a used doll, plain and simple. Harmless. With your permission, we need to take your prints, Mrs. Hudson, to exclude yours."

"Sure."

"Brawley, you didn't touch the doll, did you?"

"No, ma'am. I picked it up in the box and threw it in the backyard. But I don't believe I touched it. I probably did touch the box when I tossed it."

The younger agent took a set of prints from Brandy while they talked.

"You'll probably be relieved to know it came up negative for any toxins or explosives of any kind," she said.

Brandy found some relief in that. "Do you think this was a message? What did you call it, Brawley, a night letter?"

"Yes, a warning letter—"

"We know what a night letter is, Mr. Hanks. I'd say

that's pretty spot-on. What it does mean is that either one of the people involved in the incident in Nigeria has come here to San Diego or has talked to someone who lives here."

"So why send it?" Brandy asked.

"To scare you. And it looks like it did," the female agent answered.

"And what do we do next? We have our houses, our lives. Brawley is supposed to start a new job here in a few weeks. Are we supposed to stay in a motel room or go back to our houses and wait for the other shoe to drop?" Dorie's frustrated voice wavered.

The two agents looked at one another.

"We're not really set up with a witness protection or relocation program, not for this, anyway. We have limited resources. We can put surveillance on both houses, coordinate with the locals, have regular patrols. Maybe have someone stay with both of you, but beyond that, yes, it's a waiting game," the female agent said.

Brandy could see this was a wholly unworkable situation.

The younger agent posed the question. "Do you have family or relatives you can go stay with, either of you?"

CHAPTER 13

ON THE WAY to the airport, Coop tended to Jenna. He cleaned and put sterile pads on several surface wounds and put a strip on her cut. Kyle had Tucker drive so he could make contact with Collins. Traffic at this early hour of the morning was non-existent, except for an occasional delivery truck.

Cooper complained, so Tucker slowed down. "Sorry, man." He turned to Kyle. "You asked the jet to stay, right?".

"I did, but you never know. With a small airport in a foreign country, things happen. He could be directed off, or they charge a huge retainer for layovers."

Tucker watched Kyle switch his phone on. The small screen lit up like Christmas.

"Holy shit, Collins has been calling me every half-hour. Something's going on back home." He dialed the number and then put it on speaker. "Hope you don't mind."

There was nothing but silence in the back two seats.

Collins' voice cracked. "About fuckin' time Lansdowne. You guys okay?"

"Right as rain, and we got the package. A lot of computers and other stuff someone in Washington is going to want to take a look at."

"Okay, here's what's up. We got a big problem."

Tucker held his breath. He could see T.J. and Fredo had pulled themselves awake and were hanging over the seat. Cooper held Jenna against him, wrapped in a blanket. She was drinking a bottle of water.

"Hey, Collins, I've got you on speaker. I've got half the team in the van, just so you know."

"That's okay. Everyone needs to know. Last night, I got a call from Brawley. Someone delivered a package to Tucker's house, and Brandy opened it."

Tucker squeezed the steering wheel and shouted, "Is she okay?"

"Yes, yes, she's safe. They're all safe."

Tucker sighed with relief.

"Who is they, Collins?" asked Kyle.

"Brawley, Dorie, the little one and Brandy got moved to the Marriott until we could inspect the package, and check out both the houses. Inside the box was a doll with a hand cut off."

"Fuckin' perverts," Fredo barked.

Tucker's mind was winding around itself. He tried to grasp for answers he couldn't find.

"So, they're attacking at home, then," said Kyle. "They're in San Diego."

"The girls must be scared out of their gourds," said Tucker.

"Actually," sighed Collins, "I've been told the girls are pretty good. This morning a team from NCIS came over to get some information. They've just started working over the doll. It's been handled by everyone under the sun, and so far, we've got nothing."

"You getting us home this morning? That better be a yes, Collins." asked Kyle.

"I wanted to hear from you first, but yes, I'll make sure the jet is there. Does the girl need any medical attention? Should she go to a hospital? Or, I could find a private clinic."

"I think she's good till we're stateside," said Cooper. "You know, the usual testing for what she's been through."

"I want to go home!" Jenna shouted.

"Under the circumstances, Collins, we need to get off this island as soon as is possible," added Kyle. "One thing you'll need to arrange for us is a passport for Jenna. They'll check ours at the airport. In her condition, and she's a little beat up, I don't want to involve the local authorities. That would be a ticket for a week's delay, or worse."

"I'm on it. So what about the Dutchman and his body guards?"

"All but two are done. It was very quiet and quick. We left everything the way we found it, but took the laptops and cell phones, which ought to be a treasure trove," reported Kyle.

"Okay, well, I've got some calls to make. I'll be in touch. You guys head for the airport. What's your ETA?"

"Two, two and a half hours."

Tucker needed to be in touch with Brandy. "Collins, I gotta call my wife."

"You better, or you'll be getting a divorce next month," quipped Collins.

"And does Christy know?" asked Kyle.

"Yeah, she was the first one I called. Solid as a rock, but she'll want to hear it from you. Tucker, all of you, go ahead and call your families to give them a heads-up. We don't want anyone opening up packages."

Tucker didn't know what this country's laws were, but since it was night, he doubted anyone would catch him on the phone. Brandy picked up at the first ring.

"Tucker! Thank God. Is everything okay?"

"Comin' home, baby. You hang on."

"Listen, the Navy guys thought perhaps we should drive up to stay with Brawley's folks in Oregon."

"That's a no, Brandy. I'm going to be home in a day."

"But shouldn't we leave the area?"

"Maybe your dad's, but no long road trips. Absolutely not."

"Brawley and Dorie really want to go."

"I think it's a bad idea. You stay right where you are until I come. No moving around. Stay put and let everyone do their jobs."

Tucker knew they'd lose control if everyone scattered in different directions. And if something should happen, it would be too hard to get there in time. They were better off as a unit, families and all. He cursed the investigators for having put the idea into their heads.

One by one, each of the men talked to their wives and families. Coop let Jenna briefly talk to her father, who was screaming for joy.

Tucker wound through the city center, where traffic became congested, though dawn was still several hours away. Most of the congestion was due to large vans and early shop deliveries. There wasn't a building above three stories, and most of them looked at least two-hundred years old. With no public streetlamps, the going was slow, and Tucker had to be on guard for motorbikes and small lorries that buzzed in and around traffic like motorcycles did on the California freeways. By the time they came to the two-lane approach to the airport, Tucker's armpits were drenched, and he was reminded he'd not showered like some of the other men had.

He mulled over and over in his mind how the elements they'd fought against in Nigeria had been able to infiltrate their border. Could this militia group be more mobile than they assumed? In all his years of service, it was the first time consequences of his actions over in the arena actually followed him home. Or the first time that he knew of.

They'd not talked about their last job except to their liaison, and Kyle did most of the coordination with the CIA and prepared their formal mission papers, which were on file with the Navy. Yet something had slipped through the cracks.

He wondered if he should call Brawley but figured he wouldn't be so stupid as to take off with the family. But he wasn't the SOF Command's responsibility any longer. He was in that limbo land between having been formally detached from the Team and not yet picked up elsewhere. Tucker decided to wait, perhaps give his best friend a call when his boss wasn't sitting right next to him.

He was grateful, nonetheless, in the wisdom of getting Brandy out of the house and finding her the safe place to spend the night. Brawley would fully protect her; of that he was sure.

The Jeep passed them by, so Tucker followed them all the way to a gated entrance near the hangar. The sentry made note of the sticker in the driver side window, and they were allowed to enter the secure compound. The gate closed behind them. Tucker parked right next to the other vehicle. Kelly dashed from the passenger side to check on Jenna, who was being helped out by Cooper.

But the jet was nowhere on the tarmac and not on the horizon. Tucker doubted that they'd land now until morning, but hopefully it wasn't too far away.

"What do you think?" Sven asked him.

"I don't think they can land at night. But I guess it depends on the bird," Tucker answered. They all stood in a huddle, waiting for instructions.

Kelly got off her phone. "Good news. Mr. Riley has made the arrangements for a backup plane, in case they can't cut the other one loose. It will take about three hours to arrive," Kelly said to Kyle. "We can wait in the Net Jet building until we know. There's food and coffee in there."

Kyle directed the team to unload everything from the vehicles and deposit their things inside the hangar.

"I imagine he must be one happy fella," Tucker said to the special agent.

"That phone call from Jenna will be something he remembers for the rest of his life. He's greatly indebted to you all."

Kyle stepped up. "We're supposed to get a passport for Jenna. You don't happen to have one, do you?"

"I do not. But perhaps her father has a copy we could get delivered. You want me to try?"

"Wouldn't hurt. Collins is working to arrange it, but that could take a while. You got any other Department contacts here on the island?"

"Nobody I trust. I think your man is our best bet, but let me see if we can get a copy of the original one."

She sat Jenna down in the middle of the group. Except for a handful of staffers preparing food and stocking vending machines, the place was empty. From several paces away, she made another call and then waited. About ten minutes later, her phone pinged with a message. "Got it!" she shouted to Kyle.

"Thank God. I hope it's enough."

Tucker was looking for someone official. "If the jet arrives, maybe we just board and forget the permission."

"Never happen. As soon as the plane lands, customs will be here in a flash," answered Sven. "They're notified of incoming."

Kyle sent the picture of the passport to Collins for added ammunition.

A large black van stopped at the gated sentry and was allowed in. The seals on the sides doors were not readable, but it was apparent an official of some kind had arrived. Before the two suited gentlemen got to the entrance of the hangar, they could hear the buzzing of a plane overhead.

Kelly Fielding introduced herself and showed her credentials. The gray-haired gentleman with the large moustache gave her a long perusal before he decided to show his identification. He spoke in Spanish, and Kelly continued in the same.

Kyle stood next to Fredo to get an unofficial translation.

"They're asking about the girl."

"Uh oh," whispered Kyle.

Kelly showed the man a copy of Jenna's passport, and then she said something quietly Fredo couldn't hear. He took a picture of the passport image with his own phone and walked away to make a phone call.

The jet, twice the size of the first one, landed with a boom and then taxied until it got within a hundred yards of the building. Tucker could make out two pilots, who waited.

A stretch Mercedes with diplomatic flags appeared at the sentry gate and was granted entry. The two officials jogged over to greet whomever was sitting in the back seat.

"Not sure about this," said Kyle.

Sven shrugged his shoulders. "I'd be more concerned if it was a troop transport truck. I think we're about to be given the golden ticket."

The older official bowed, gave a salute to whomever was in the vehicle, and headed back to the hangar.

The Mercedes, with its mysterious passenger turned around and left the compound.

In broken English, the gentleman with the moustache spoke to their group. "We have been given assurances by the Brazilian Consulate General in person that your papers are in order. He was entrusted to get everything ready, but he apologizes for the delay. He says it was all his fault. And he's promised us he will deliver the necessary documents to my office this morning. So you are free to go."

Tucker exchanged stares with Sven.

Kyle monitored a text that pinged his phone. "Collins," he said, waving the screen in the air.

The two officials were on their way back to their car.

"That sonofabitch," Kyle whispered, shaking his head. "The old man came through for us."

The bags were loaded aboard the plane with haste. Kyle remained on the tarmac while everyone else boarded the gangway. He waved to the officials standing beside their car, boarded the plane, spoke to the pilots, and then took the first vacant seat in front.

Tucker sat behind Sven. As the plane began to taxi, Cooper called out, "Just where are we off to?"

"Norfolk. We'll be on US soil in ten hours."

CHAPTER 14

"**H**E SAID NOT to go, Brawley." Brandy had pleaded with them not to leave. "They're on their way home. Just wait. One more day," she pleaded.

"Brandy, we don't know if we're any safer here than in our own home," said Dorie.

"Well, first of all, there's no evidence that they even made it to your home. And secondly, this is a big hotel. The Navy knows we're here. I believe Collins. This is the safest place we could be, like he told you."

Jessica had been fussy all morning, and Brandy could see it was stressing Dorie out. Without her toys and her regular routine, keeping a toddler amused in a hotel room was next to impossible.

"Why don't you take her for a swim?" she suggested. "There's a big indoor pool here."

"How is that any safer?" Brawley spat.

"I didn't bring my suit," mumbled Dorie. "Look, if we just left now, we could be up past Eugene in ten, twelve hours. About the time they land. And they still have to catch a flight to California after that. His folks' place is like a bunker. Nothing could touch us there."

Tucker had told her the stories. Brawley's dad had been a SEAL, on the teams over twenty years before retirement. She imagined he'd have enough firepower for an independence movement.

"You really should come with us, Brandy. It's the smart thing to do," Brawley insisted.

"I'm doing what Tucker asked. I'm going to stay right here."

It sucked that there was no protocol, no procedure for these types of situations. Her husband was unreachable again. If she stayed with one of the other wives, she might bring attention to them as well. It wasn't safe, but there was no definite plan. The hardest thing for her to do right now was wait.

Dorie and Brawley were showering and preparing for their trip, which would leave Brandy without a vehicle, but she didn't mind about that. She was more worried about being left all alone. She decided to give Christy a call.

"I'm glad you called. I got a chance to talk to Kyle and they're on the plane. Won't be long now. How are you holding up?"

"Christy, I'm wondering if I'm doing the right thing."

"You mean about the house?"

"Oh God no!" She found herself giggling despite herself. "About waiting here. I feel like a sitting duck."

"But they're checking in. You know they are."

"Yes, that's what we were told. The NCIS guys were not very reassuring."

"I wish they'd let you come to my place, but I've been told not to. I think that's smart, too."

"Yes, it's the right thing."

"There really isn't any alternative, Brandy."

"Well, Brawley and Dorie are driving up to his folks place in Oregon. They think that's the safest right now."

"But you're supposed to stay together and stay put."

"I am, but they're leaving, Christy. Nothing I can do to change their minds."

"Dammit."

"Should I go with them?"

"No. Please, Brandy, just stay there. There won't be any help if you leave the protection of the motel and the people they have watching over you. You don't see them, but I'm sure they're there. You have to trust in that."

"I'll be all alone."

"What about your father?"

"I can't involve him. To be honest, I'd feel safer

with Brawley. At least he can shoot."

"Well, there is that. But you have a gun, don't you?"

"We brought some of Tucker's. He's trained me on his SigSauer, enough so I know how to use it without shooting myself. If I'm left alone, I'm more likely to shoot the housekeeping staff if I get too spooked."

Her eyes began watering. The whole situation was confusing and dangerous. There was no leader, no one's instructions to follow, except the man who was fifteen hours or more away.

"Look, I've got to go check on the kids. Keep your cool. Call me as often as you like. We can stay connected that way. I'll let you know if I hear anything, and you do the same. Okay?"

"Okay. Thanks, Christy."

"I'm here for you. If I didn't have the kids, I'd be right beside you with my .38. And you know I can shoot too."

The call cheered her slightly. But then the quietness of the room descended upon her. She took their breakfast tray to the door, checked the hallway to make sure it was deserted, flipped the doorstop, and laid the tray to the side. Again, surveying the area, she listened. It was quiet, too quiet. There was absolutely no sign of anyone guarding them.

"Is anyone there?" she called out. After several seconds, she repeated the question. "Anybody out there?"

Her answer was complete silence, which confirmed her suspicion. No one was on guard, watching out for her and her growing family.

Closing the door, she sat on her bed and made a decision.

Brawley stepped through the adjoining opening. "We're ready to go. Last chance, Brandy. I still think I'm your best bet."

She looked up at him and nodded. "I'm ready. I've decided."

"Smart cookie," he said as he winked.

They again struggled with the bags, Brawley taking the heavy ones and loading Brandy's suitcase with the diaper bag and Dorie's soft shoulder satchel. As before, she held Jessica and the rolling suitcase while Dorie helped Brawley with the duty bags.

She almost left behind her phone charger and managed to run back in before the door closed for the final time.

They walked through the lobby area, filled with guests waiting to check out and a girls' soccer team waiting to check in. Brandy nearly tripped over a bright yellow ball that was skimming over the granite tile floor.

The valet brought the truck and helped load the heavy bags into the bed. Brawley gave them twenty dollars, and with Dorie in back with Jessica, Brandy sat up front with Brawley. They were off.

Instead of heading for the interstate, Brawley doubled back onto the island.

"What are you doing?"

"I'm picking up a few things Dorie needs for Jessica. Some toys, some extra diapers, and snacks. You know, stuff."

"But we could buy those on the road," Brandy protested.

"Which would take more time. This is simple. We'll just be in and out in five minutes."

Brawley knew she was fuming inside.

"And if you need a little courage," he flipped open the glove box in front of her knees, "this should do the trick."

She could see the butt of a snub-nosed revolver. "I'm not trained on this," she said in shock. .

"Don't need to be. It's loaded with five rounds. You just point and shoot. You do know how to do that, don't you?"

"You know I do."

All this discussion of guns made her nervous. She quietly closed the lid of the box and tried to calm her nerves. She found herself observing everything as they made their way to the house. Two cars passed by while Brawley was pulling into the driveway. Several other vehicles were parked in the street: A green and white landscape truck, a yellow VW Beetle, and a bright green compact pickup with something tied to the back.

She remained in the car while Brawley and Dorie dashed to the house. Jessica had already fallen asleep in her car seat.

"Just you and me, kid. Off on an adventure. Sure wish we were on our way to Disneyland or some place fun, instead of running away to 'The Compound.' Tucker had made fun of Mr. Hanks' game trophies, which covered most of the available walls in the living area. He even had several in their bedroom. He'd told her about when they used to shoot at them with their dart guns and, later on, B.B. guns. On more than one occasion, Brawley had gotten a spanking so hard he couldn't sit down for a couple of days.

"What have I gotten myself into?" she asked to the cab.

At last, the couple came from the house with another suitcase and a large what looked like a baseball bag with a logo she didn't recognize. Dorie also brought another soft beach bag and waddled along next to Brawley. Brandy noticed how pregnant she looked.

The suitcase had to go in the bed of the truck next to Brandy's. Brawley was able to stash the ball bag behind the second seat. Dorie clutched her satchel on her knees, climbing into the rear seat next to the still-sleeping Jessica.

"My dad used to say when we'd go camping, 'If it's not in the car, we don't own it.' That pretty much sums up how light we pack," Brawley boomed.

Dorie sighed. "Brawley, quiet. You'll wake her and hurry up. I'm getting the creeps sitting here. Let's get on the road."

Traffic was light since they were between commute runs. They made good time for the next two hours until the truck needed gas and Dorie wanted to get something healthy for lunch. Once again, Brandy stayed behind with Jessica while her two friends went inside to pay for the gas and make their purchases. The truck stop teemed with customers, creating a small line for gas. Brandy counted and observed cars coming and going. Something caught her eye, but as she turned and scrutinized the parking lot, she didn't find anything of interest. After gassing up, they were on their way again.

"Does your dad know we're coming?" she asked Brawley.

"Yup. They're pretty excited too. You've never been there, have you?"

"No, but I've heard a lot about it."

"Dad retired at thirty-eight. I'll be a couple of years older when I retire, God willing."

"How did he manage to be on a west coast team and live in Oregon?"

"He didn't at first. Then when he met my mom, well her Mennonite roots are here in Oregon. They bought a place up there when I was born. My mom's kin thought they'd make a farmer out of him. It didn't take."

"I can imagine. Your mom doesn't drink, is that right?"

"No coffee, smoking, alcohol. I'm sure it surprised most of his friends when they hooked up."

"So they bought a farm and he still deployed. I'll bet you missed him."

"I honestly don't remember. The last six years he stayed down here during the week and came home most weekends, and we did stuff the whole time. There are always lots of guys who do that, lots of divorced guys who room together. I think he also saw that my mom wouldn't fit into the wives' club, if you know what I mean."

"She seems nice, Brawley."

"Fiercely loyal but definitely an acquired taste, like my dad."

Brandy appreciated the light-hearted conversation and, for a few minutes, forgot the peril they were running from. The farther and farther away from San Diego they got, the more she began to relax.

Maybe Tucker wouldn't approve of her decision, but she definitely felt it was way easier on the nerves.

Plus, being beside another man of action, someone she'd known well and knew would do anything to defend his turf and his ladies, brought comfort to her soul. It was just one long road trip. By the time they got up to Oregon, Tucker would be only a few hours from home.

And then everything would be perfect again. She knew he'd figure out a way to make her feel safe.

CHAPTER 15

SVEN TURNED AROUND in his seat to address Tucker. "You still mad?"

"Yes." Tucker glanced out the window, studying the blackness and the grey clouds hovering above the ocean. He was going to hold it over Sven for as long as he could get away with it.

But what was the point? It was going to be a long flight, and the mission had been accomplished, which was the most important thing.

"No," he murmured, still not making eye contact.

Sven quickly slipped from his seat to the one next to Tucker. "Didn't take you for holding grudges."

Tucker glared at him. "Wasn't there another way? Did you have to go all Spygate on us? Do you know what that could have cost?"

Sven's blue eyes smiled even if the rest of his face didn't. "That was my idea. I wanted the plane to be in the air first."

"We could have turned around."

"Sure, but you know that wouldn't happen."

"So you weren't sure if we'd abort if we knew all the connection? See, we do things differently on our team. We trust each other."

Sven punched him gently in the arm. "I trust you all day every day. I don't trust your government. I don't trust the upper crust of your Navy. Remember, we're the 'little country' people. We get squashed. We're careful."

"So get the big brown bear angry and then watch him take out the whole block."

"Pretty much, yes."

"Well, you've had your bite. Don't ever do that to me again. I'm not so sure there is a place for you on our team, in case you were thinking about it. We just don't do this to each other. We die for each other. Don't take my life for granted, and I won't take yours."

Sven held out his hand for a shake. Tucker took it, and they both looked off in opposite directions.

The Norwegian kept prodding. "It sounds like you have some problems at home. Something about a doll delivered to your wife? What's that about?"

"It surprised me. I'm trying to figure out how those assholes in Nigeria came to find us in San Diego."

"It's been all over the news. Your border?"

"Don't remind me. We could fix it. Everyone just

has to learn to talk to each other without picking fights." Tucker didn't really want to talk politics. But it came out anyway.

"So let's think carefully. You honestly believe someone from that group flew over to the US and lay in wait for you or your wife? They would have had to know where you came from, even what team you were on. I'm not sure even Jean's people knew all that information. Not that they couldn't have found it."

Tucker thought he had a point and nodded his agreement.

"So the second-best explanation is that someone who is sympathetic to their cause actually lives in San Diego or nearby. Someone they could have talked to by phone."

"But again, they would have to know where we were stationed," Tucker posed.

"Unless they were already there. What if they were positioned there not for you specifically, but because it was close to the Naval base? What if that was the intended eventual target, and you guys just walked on stage?"

"You mean like a sleeper cell?" Tucker asked.

"Exactly that. Can you tell me if incidences like these are more or less frequent?" Sven waited eagerly for Tucker's answer.

But Tucker didn't have to say a word. Then the

question popped up again.

"Sven, how exactly did we 'walk on stage' as you say?"

The Norwegian shrugged. "I have no idea. I wasn't there. You were, though. Because they targeted you."

After several minutes, the two warriors fell asleep.

SUNLIGHT MOVED THROUGH the portal window as the jet banked left and lowered altitude. It roused Tucker from a dream he was having. He kept hearing the words, *she'll make a man out of you!* over and over again. Laughter fluttered all around him. He remembered laughing too, holding his belly.

Immediately, he sat up. He remembered exactly the event that triggered the dream. It was his conversation with Jackie Daniels at the flea market in San Diego.

"Holy shit!" he whispered.

Sven opened one bloodshot eye nastily. "Excuse me?"

"I remember now. I think I know how I got singled out. Excuse me, Sven. I gotta talk to Kyle."

Sven stood and repositioned himself across the aisle in a vacant row. Tucker dashed to the front of the plane. Kyle was asleep, his legs resting on the pair of leather chairs in front of him. He slipped onto one of the seats and touched Kyle's right knee.

His LPO jerked awake. "What the hell?" When he

saw Tucker, he relaxed back, rubbing his eyes.

"What time is it?"

"I think it's about zero-five-hundred. But, Kyle, I remember something that might be helpful."

"Shoot. I think I'm awake."

"You remember that day when we went down to the flea market with Brawley? Fredo bought those soccer balls and everyone was making fun of him?"

"Yeah. I remember."

"We met up with Jackie Daniels?"

"Okay, yes. What's up with that?"

"Do you remember I told him I'd gotten married—"

"And you slapped your belly, and he told you it would make you a man—" Kyle interrupted.

"—and Brawley told Jackie's girls he was a war hero and we all cheered for him?" Tucker completed.

"That's what happened. Someone overheard. It was someone from the flea market. Tucker, they must have followed you home."

"That's exactly what I think happened. They waited until we weren't home and left the package at the doorstep. Could have bought that old doll there somewhere too."

"Totally makes sense, Tucker. They targeted you because they saw you talking with Jackie." Kyle stared back up at him a vein in his forehead thumping. "Wonder if Jackie is in any danger."

"We gotta talk to him. We gotta tell the NCIS."

Over the next few minutes, both Kyle and Tucker questioned the other men who that day were there, asking if they remembered any of the crowd around them at the flea market, particularly their faces. Everyone remembered the incident, but no one recalled their audience.

But they all agreed that Jackie might. As a frequent attendee of the swap meets and flea markets in the area, his eyes might pick up something the rest of them would overlook.

TUCKER HAD BEEN told the plane would be given special clearance for landing at Norfolk, since they were on an official mission. They were also warned that the next leg wouldn't have them sitting in such luxury.

Kyle was on the phone with Collins, who would relay the message to Jackie, not only to ask for his help in finding whomever might have left the package, but for a heads-up for his own family's health and safety. The two men were still on the phone when Tucker decided to call Brandy.

"Tucker!" she answered. "Are you back on US soil?"

"I sure am. Can't wait to get home. How's the Marriott?"

He heard a pause at the other end of the line.

"Brandy?"

"Um, Tucker, I didn't do what you asked. I'm so sorry. But I'm with Brawley and Dorie. We're headed to Oregon. We're nearly halfway there, just left the Sacramento area."

"What?" Tucker gripped the cell so hard he actually saw the case bend in his hand.

"I decided to stay with them, to stay together. I didn't want to be alone in that hotel. Figured I'd be safer with Brawley."

"No, no, no! Dammit, Brandy. How am I going to get to you?"

"You can take a plane to"—he waited while she conferred with Brawley—"He says Salem would be the closest. You let us know, and we'll come pick you up."

"Put Brawley on the line." Tucker was ready to explode.

"Hey, glad you're back, bud."

"You fuckin' asshole. I asked her to stay put where they could keep an eye on her."

"Wait a minute, Tucker. You're exaggerating it all out of proportion. We're fine. We've had a very whole day on the road. We've been able to gas up, get food. Everyone's happy, Tuck. No stress here."

"Brawley, can you put this on speaker?" Tucker begged.

"It's not synced, but yes we've got you on speaker now. Brandy's holding the phone up so we all can hear."

"We're working on a couple of leads, but we don't

have anything definite yet. Just clues, places we're starting. We think we know the source. What that means for all of you is that you have to be very, very savvy about what's going on around you at all times. Don't make any unnecessary stops, don't go shopping or wander away from each other or away from other people. Don't allow strangers to get close to your car or to strike up a conversation. Keep your distance from everyone but stay in populated areas. You don't want to be caught alone anywhere, in case you're being followed."

"You really think this could be happening?"

Tucker couldn't believe Brawley was still in denial. "Always possible, Brawley. Until we find someone to detain. Please, please be careful. Since you're halfway up there, I won't demand you return to San Diego, but you took a big risk streaking out on your own. Brawley, you weren't smart."

"Look, Tucker, that's B.S. First, we don't really know if someone's trying to cause us harm or just scare us. And they've done that. Best we're out of the way completely so you guys can tear up the houses or lay in wait for a suspect to do something. But let's be clear. No one has been harmed yet."

"Yet," repeated Tucker.

"When do you arrive in San Diego?"

"Early in the morning. Before sunlight. We're waiting for our flight now."

Brandy cleared her throat. Tucker felt the strain in

her words. "Tucker, I'm sorry. I was so scared. There was no one to talk to. I didn't see any of the people they said would be watching over us. I felt like I was totally exposed, and I had to take the only option I felt comfortable with. Please, it wasn't an easy decision to make, sweetheart."

"I understand." Her words melted some of his anger, and he softened his voice. "I'm frustrated, too, because there's nothing I can do. You probably made the right decision, in hindsight. Brawley will guard you with his life, as I would all of you. Just pay attention. Be smart from here on until I get there and we have this figured out and catch someone."

"Thank you for understanding, Tucker."

"Always, Brandy. I don't want anything to happen to you. Any of you."

He let that sink in, hoping they understood the gravity of the problem ahead of them. But then Brawley spoiled it.

"Any other tips you wish to share with us?" he said flippantly. Before Tucker could respond, Brawley quickly apologized. "Okay, that was unfair."

"Damn right. I'll call back when we're back in San Diego. Go straight to Oregon. Don't veer from the path. Stay together."

"We will," Brandy agreed.

Tucker added, "One more thing. Stay armed."

CHAPTER 16

N O ONE SAID a word as the day turned into evening. The I-5 California freeway was nearly deserted. Weather was dry and had started to cool from the heat of the day. They'd been on the road twelve hours when they came to the town of Redding, which lay at the bottom of the Shasta summit, a long desolate stretch of the highway very treacherous in the winter. But without rain or snow, it was easy for Brawley to go over ninety miles an hour, as he had during much of the I-5 stretch.

Brandy had switched seats with Dorie, who talked to keep Brawley awake. She was rooting for having them stay overnight some place, but Brawley was not having any of it.

Jessica had been chattering and awake for a large portion of the trip. They'd let her run around at their various pit stops before the call with Tucker. Now that they had been warned, their stops were quick and efficient.

But thankfully, Jessica was sound asleep when Brawley announced he needed to get gas and the large truck stop just south of Redding was full of truckers and cars going in both directions, clean rest rooms with showers, and a huge restaurant serving home-made pie. It was a trucker's haven where they could use the internet, rent a computer and printer, drop off or pick up music CDs, videos and audiotapes. It even had a self-serve laundry and a twenty-four-hour diesel mechanic. So at midnight, it was probably the busiest stop between Sacramento and Eugene.

"How's your bladder?" Dorie asked her.

"Probably not as bad as yours is. You go first. Both of you go. I'll stay in the car with Jessica."

Brawley handed her the keys. The couple walked arm in arm to the restaurant as Brandy adjusted herself, anxious to get out and stretch. But, as promised, she kept the windows and doors locked.

She should have told them to have a shower, a little alone intimate time together. She knew Dorie could use some warm water and loving kisses. Brawley was probably stiff as a board from all the driving. He was as stubborn as Tucker was and, though Brandy had offered several times, refused to even take a short nap, allowing someone else to drive.

She looked at her feet and found a plastic bottle

with about an inch of water left. She sipped it down then allowed her hips to slide over the vinyl seat so her head could rest on the back. Her knees hit Dorie's bucket seat ahead of her. She planned on taking a long, long nap and then volunteer to spell Dorie again so she could do her part to keep Brawley awake and mentally occupied. The energy drinks he was knocking down practically non-stop were helping, but soon, he was going to have to get some real rest. She guessed he'd be purchasing some 5-Hour Energy concentrate inside.

Cars lined up on one side of the pumps, the large rigs on the other. Occasionally, an idiot driver would take up a whole lane and make the huge trucks wait for him to get his diesel from the truck side. But by and large, it was an orderly transition with people washing the bugs off their windshields and checking their tire pressure in between their fill ups. There was a drive-through vehicle wash in both sizes—one for trucks and one for passenger vehicles, which was operating non-stop.

While Brandy watched a couple of truckers with matching beer bellies sharing a soda, and waiting for their rigs to fill, a bright green truck with a black carpenter's rack pulled ahead and parked parallel to Brawley's truck. Two lanky youths exited the truck and peered at the restaurant with binoculars, sharing them back and forth, pointing.

She'd seen that truck before, she was sure of it. Blinking several times, she finally remembered seeing it on Brawley's block when the two of them were inside gathering their additional things before the trip. What were the odds the same identical truck would be way up here in Redding, stopped at the same rest stop?

The odds were too great to calculate.

She tried to dial Brawley, but he didn't pick up. When she dialed Dorie's phone, the cell chirped in the front of the cab. With barely any battery left she tried to dial 911 and her phone died before it could connect.

She continued to watch the men as she started to type a text to Brawley, but again her phone's screen went black. Then one of them pulled a rifle from the cab and balanced it on the roof. He was lining up a shot.

Brandy knew she only had seconds. Scrambling, she nearly fell from the back seat, gripped the passenger side door handle, ripped it open, and lunged into the front of the cab. She pressed on the glove box, and it didn't open. She used a fist and banged on the metal flap. Again, although it was now dented, it didn't open.

Jessica was stirring. She was directly in the line of sight between the youth with the rifle and the toddler. She'd have to distract him, make herself a target to keep Jessica safe. She took a darting glance at the restaurant entrance and still didn't see Dorie or Brawley.

One last time, she kicked the glove box, and finally, it gaped open like the tongue of a robot. She clutched the police special and found it lighter than she was used to. Her hands were shaking so hard she nearly dropped it on the asphalt.

The youth with the rifle was using his scope, fixing on something inside the restaurant. With adrenaline pumping full force, almost enough to make her explode, she held the gun at her side, like she'd seen Tucker do many times.

"Hey!" she yelled, moving to the right, waving her arms above her head. "Are you looking for me?"

Several pedestrians nearby scurried out of the way, and one woman shrieked and ran inside the building, dropping packages behind her.

The two boys whipped around to face her. Their eyes squinted in the overhead lights. The boy on the right began to reach behind him. The one on the left repositioned his rifle—bringing it up to his eye, taking slow, careful aim—while the other began running directly toward her and briefly blocked the shot. She knew what the kid was reaching for because she was doing the same thing herself. But she'd practiced this many times at the shooting range with Tucker. She'd shot with the other wives when they first were dating. It all came surging back to her.

With a last glance at the building's entrance, she took one more leap to the right, away from the truck, raised Brawley's police special from her side, just as she saw the revolver appear in his right hand. Brandy aimed slightly low to the boy's body mass, preparing for recoil like she'd been trained, and pulled the trigger.

She heard Brawley scream and items hit the pavement, but she didn't see him. Her focus was on the trajectory of her round, which lodged in the boy's forehead. The kid with the rifle took a quick shot in her direction, but it went wide to her right and cracked a windshield behind her. Brandy returned fire, and again, her aim was true. It caught him right in the center of his chest, and he dropped.

That's when she heard the screaming, and for a second, she wondered what they were yelling at. Someone tackled her hard, but he was soon pulled off by the angry Brawley, who drew her to his chest in a tight bearhug. She leaned against him like a limp rag and tried to breathe. On the third try, she squeaked, with just enough energy to punch Brawley in the chest.

"I can't breathe!" she gasped, and immediately, he released the pressure, but kept his arms wrapped around her, not letting her fall.

That first delicious inhale felt so good. Then everything turned black.

CHAPTER 17

TUCKER GOT THE call as soon as they landed in San Diego. Sven told him Riley had secured a private jet to get him up to Redding as fast as possible. Collins confirmed the Navy granted him the time to go bring Brandy back. Kelly and Jenna had arrived in Portland for the reunion with a very grateful Mr. Riley.

Brawley met him at the Redding Jetway terminal alone. He explained his wife and daughter were at the hospital with Brandy.

"When you're up to it, Tucker—"

"I'm not up to it."

"She was amazing. Talk about grace under fire. Just sayin'."

"Not fuckin' now."

Tucker had been told about the shootout, of course. He didn't doubt for one minute she was capable of heroic behavior, but he still needed to see her for himself. He knew she would be okay, but he wanted to make sure she understood that this would never happen again. He never wanted her to be in harm's way like this.

He'd done lots of thinking during his long plane trips home and was on the verge of making some big decisions, based on Brandy's frame of mind. He was done with the texting, the Facetime calls, the writing in journals to let her read perhaps some day after he was dead. He was done with it all.

Everything revolved around her. If something had happened to her, if she'd sacrificed herself to save Jessica or to protect Dorie or Brawley, he would be inconsolable. He'd be a shell of the man he once was. And this was too close. Way too close. He couldn't ask this of her ever again.

He and Brawley had formed a kind of mental bond during their growing up years and it was still there right now, even though they didn't say a word. He was furious at his best friend for allowing his wife to get in the middle of something she had no right to be involved in. At the same time, he knew Brawley had just done what he thought best. She was the one who chose. Thank God it worked out.

He'd loved Brawley like a brother. They shared everything together in those days playing against each other in basketball, soccer, and baseball. They shared unmentionable bad dates, and great first dates, breakups and heartaches. Brawley was there for him when he got divorced, when he thought he'd never have a woman again by his side. Now look at him. Now the both of them were expecting babies. It was another life event he shared with Brawley.

And though Brawley couldn't be on the last mission they completed, he'd been there during the first part of it. He'd gotten it kicked off. By accident, Brawley had created the bait that allowed the elimination of the bad guys.

Everything in his life was connected to Brawley. Brandy relied on him, trusted him. He'd made sure she knew where the gun was or the outcome would have been much different. Everything contributed to the result that had the possibility of a happy ending.

After all was said and done, what he thought of Brawley's decision or Brandy's lack of following directions was small potatoes compared to what was really important. They were all safe. They would make it out together, alive. Even the unborn babies would be safe. Life would go on, as long as he protected it. That's what he'd commit the rest of his life to doing.

Brawley drove carefully, as if juggling him around in the cab of his big truck would cause him to explode. But Tucker knew he wasn't that fragile. His conscience was beginning to irritate him. It was time to make his peace.

He glanced over at Brawley, who gave a tiny smile Tucker could see in profile. His eyes remained pinned to the road.

"You know what really bothers me more than anything, Brawley?"

"I think I have a pretty good idea."

"I couldn't control any of it. Not one fuckin' thing. No one did what I asked. And yet, somehow, everything worked out."

"Well, you have the little issue of a hearing on the shooting, but I think she'll be cleared, don't you?"

"I'm not even thinking about that."

"I know. I'm just as much at fault as you are, Tucker. Going all big man at the flea market. You did hear the story, didn't you?"

"I think I missed it."

"When Collins asked Jackie about that day, the terp remembered having conversations with an older couple at the flea market. They compared their immigration process. The couple made their living selling things from their West African heritage, and were very excited about becoming Americans, just like Jackie. The one thing they had a problem with were their two youngest boys, both radicalized by recent trips overseas. The boys were caught up in some false idea they were freedom fighters. He remembered they were distressed the boys were out of control. Just as they feared, the investigators found out the boys were being groomed for something very public and very big, a massive show of force against the Navy."

"I feel sad for them. How is that possible, Brawley? Does that make me a wimp?"

"Because you're a decent human being. Because you're trying to help the innocents get away from being preyed upon. If you weren't a man with honest feelings, you'd kill with a coldness that would repel anyone who knew you. You're not that guy. You care about people. And you find home with others who live as intensely as you do."

Tucker thought about all that. "You do a pretty good job of buttering someone up, Brawley."

"If you're saying you're strong enough to accept the truth about yourself, well then, yes. You could call it buttering you up."

The Redding hospital was straight ahead, perched on a hilltop overlooking the deep green valley forged by the Sacramento River. They parked near the Emergency entrance and Brawley walked Tucker past the nurses' station to the rear elevator and up to the third floor.

He stopped to address his best friend before entering Brandy's room. "For the record, Tucker, I'm sorry. I made a mistake, and it almost cost me the life of my best friend's wife. That's unforgiveable, but I'm still asking for it."

Tucker grabbed Brawley and the two hugged because there wasn't anything else that could be said or done.

"I appreciate that, Brawley. Now, tell me what I'm getting into."

Brawley put his hands on his hips. "Nope. I'm going to let you walk in cold and figure it out for yourself."

She was sleeping with Jessica tucked into her arm. Tucker didn't think he'd ever seen her so beautiful, even though it appeared she'd roughed up her face a bit. He was going to have the ass of the person who did that to her, if he was still alive.

Her long hair had been brushed and wasn't the usual tangle on the pillowcase he was used to seeing. Dorie was bent over on the wheeled table that held her water. She was also fast asleep.

He turned to let her sleep, when Brandy opened her eyes and gave him a big smile. Her expression changed as her hand came up and felt the bandage that had been placed there.

In two long strides, he was at her bedside, suddenly ashamed he hadn't brought her anything like flowers she so richly deserved.

"Hey, sweetheart," he whispered and kissed her even though she whimpered. He didn't care and kissed her harder.

Tucker positioned himself on the edge of the bed as Jessica started to stir but then found another comfortable position in Brandy's arms.

"You look so beautiful. You are so amazing, Brandy. And I'm so sorry you had to go through all this."

She was just staring up at him, tears streaming down her cheeks. "Never in a million years did I think when you taught me to shoot that I'd need that training. I really hesitated, almost didn't do it. That was what I was the most scared of. I thought, if I didn't get over this hurdle, I wouldn't live to regret anything or to see you or our daughter."

"Son."

"Whatever."

"You did good. Brawley is over-the-moon impressed with your tactical skills," he said through his chuckle.

"There was nothing tactical about it. Point and shoot."

"The decision to shoot the right person is always the biggest thing, Brandy. That's what I meant. No one else was harmed." He touched the bandage on her lip. "Who can I punish who did this?"

"Oh." She started to giggle, which woke Jessica up in earnest. Dorie rose, craned her neck, gave Tucker a hug, and took the toddler from her, exiting the room.

"It was some good Samaritan thinking he was stopping a crazed hormonal woman from shooting at her boyfriend or something. I think I chipped a tooth."

"He beat you up?"

"No, he tackled me! Knocked me unconscious."

Tucker did begin to laugh behind his hand, in spite of himself.

"It wasn't funny, Tucker," she barked.

"No, I understand. But he was being brave."

He loved the flash of anger in her eyes, that fighting spirit that wanted justice. If the gentleman hadn't knocked her out, she'd have gotten the better of him, Tucker was certain.

"I'll show you how to fend off an attacker next," he said through his laughter.

"No, don't! Because that's what will happen next. Don't you dare!" Her eyes were huge, her cheeks had pinked up, and in all her fiery loveliness, she was speaking honestly.

He loved her more today than he ever had.

"The baby's fine?"

"Yes. They said you can listen to the heartbeat again, if you want."

"Okay, let's do that," Tucker responded. He was anxious to replace all the nasty images in his mind of what she might have lived through.

An aid entered the room, bringing in a tray. "We've

got breakfast here," the young girl said.

Brandy shrugged. "They had pancakes."

The tray was set on the wheeling cart and moved closer to Brandy.

"Should I order you some?"

"I don't think so. I've had more coffee in the past ten hours than I get in a month. What I really need to do is get you home, get you in that shower, and then get you in my bed."

Brandy stared lovingly at the pancakes. "After my breakfast?"

He stood up, shaking his head.

"Mr. Hudson?" a voice from the doorway announced.

Tucker saw one of the nurses standing there.

"I have someone who would like to speak with you."

He followed the nurse to the hallway and then several doors down to a meditation room/chapel. A white-haired man in a modern, gadget-encrusted electric wheelchair sat in the aisle, his back turned.

"You wanted to speak to me, sir?" Tucker asked.

The wheelchair turned effortlessly. The disabled gentleman was disarmingly handsome, with the brightest blue eyes Tucker had ever seen. He wore an expensive deep blue suit with a designer shirt and tie. His shoes were highly polished and appeared never worn.

The man's heavily veined hands worked the controls of the electric device until he was close enough to extend his hand.

"I'm Colin Riley, Jenna's most grateful father, Mr. Hudson. Can I call you Mr. Hudson?"

Tucker shook the man's hand. He was surprised to feel the strength of Mr. Riley's firm handshake.

"Of course, Mr. Riley. Nice to meet you too."

Several other things began to surface as Colin Riley started speaking. He was measured. His eyes were friendly and warm but far from weak. Tucker could even say that the man was driven.

"Sit down, Mr. Hudson. I won't take much of your time." He smiled. "I know this is a special day, as mine was yesterday, and I have you to thank for that."

"It was our job, really. I'm not the team leader. That would be Kyle Lansdowne."

"Yes, I'm well aware of that. But you had more skin in the game, shall we say."

Tucker bristled at this a bit. "Sir?"

"It's a vulgar term, I admit, especially since you nearly lost your wife completing this mission. Many important games in business use athletic competitions to characterize them. I'm going to have to learn a more appropriate way to describe them."

Tucker's intuition was firing red hot. He wasn't

sure which ledger of the scale the man sat. But one thing was evident. He was an extremely powerful man and was used to wielding it.

"Just what did you want to speak to me about? I'd like to get back to my wife, if you don't mind."

"I wanted to thank you in person."

"Well, you've done that, sir. We just did our job."

"No, you did my job."

Again, the hackles on the back of Tucker's neck began to stand up.

"Excuse me, Mr. Riley?"

"You did a very personal task for me, even though, technically, you work for the United States Navy. I helped with some of the logistics, but I would not have used these resources if it weren't for the fact that my very foolish daughter had followed in the footsteps of her unfortunate and equally foolish brother. She's flawed. But she's all I have left. Other than my billions, of course."

Tucker was getting annoyed with how heavily laced with power and privilege his conversation was. It wasn't an arena he was familiar, nor was he comfortable with.

"You trying to impress me, Mr. Riley? Because billions of dollars don't impress me. People do. And bad people motivate me to want to squish them like a bug, like a pimple on freedom's ass."

Colin Riley beamed, his eyes filling with water. "I've grossly underestimated you, Mr. Hudson."

"Whatever," Tucker said, finally at his limit. "Look, I'm glad it turned out. I'm happy you're reunited and sorry for the loss of your son. Now I gotta leave, and I'm not going to argue anymore with you. My wife is the most valuable thing in my life, and that's where I'm going."

Tucker turned around and stormed out of the chapel. He could hear the wheelchair whining behind him. He wasn't going to stop for anything. His hands balled into fists.

"Mr. Hudson, please take my card," Tucker finally heard.

He didn't bother to turn around. "No thanks, sir."

"What if someone paid you to go take care of those bugs and made it so you never had to worry about money again?"

Tucker stopped. Wheelchair or no, he was about to deck the guy, stomp on his nice blue suit, and rip some of his hair out. He inhaled deeply three times and then faced the man again.

"One last time, Mr. Riley. My services are not for sale. The U.S. Navy owns my ass. They trained me and believed in me, twice now. They've given me a job I wake up loving to do each and every day. I get insurance. My wife's pregnancy is covered, I'm covered, the kids will get college paid for if I die, and I own my life."

He lunged forward, his face not more than a foot away from Mr. Riley's face. The man was still smiling in rapt adulation, and Tucker wanted to smack the smile right off his mug.

"I *own* my life."

Riley sat still, raised his hand and presented his card.

"We have much to discuss, Mr. Hudson. And much to learn from each other. I suggest you think about it. You can have all that and your dignity and your soul and your profession. Let me help."

Tucker ripped the card from the man's fingers, whipped around, and headed through the doors to Brandy's ward.

Brawley and Dorie were standing at the nurse's station, watching them bounce and play with Jessica. His best friend took one look at Tucker's expression and stood to full attention.

Tucker ignored them, addressing the nurses. "Can I take my wife home, *now*?"

CHAPTER 18

THE LAST OF their boxes were loaded into the driveway. The college kids they'd hired were happy with the sandwiches and the extra twenty dollars Brandy gave them apiece. She promised to let them know when they had a work party to rid the yard of much of the shrubbery, which gave privacy but ate up too much territory. She wanted a play structure, a nice perimeter fence for both the front and back yards, and a lawn. She wanted a puppy for the baby to play with some day. Her list of plans for this house was never-ending.

Dorie was nearing her term as Brandy was just beginning to show. Ever since the close of escrow, the two friends had been busy wallpapering one of the bedrooms for the nursery and painting the kitchen and most of the rest of the house. But Dorie wasn't going to be available any longer. Getting up and down a ladder was becoming too much of a risk.

Brandy drew up sketches of what she wanted the front of the house to look like and what the rooms would look like with their very sparse furniture. She calculated and planned for future buys when things went on sale. She scoured the free used furniture listings and picked up some nice finds.

Tucker arrived with drawer pulls, towel bars and new light fixtures from one of the big home improvement stores.

"Got some things I think you'll like," he said as he passed by her with his shopping bags, giving her a peck on the cheek.

"Oh, show me!"

He brought the new hardware into the kitchen and spread everything out on the old Formica countertop. "This old stuff is kind of growing on me, Brandy," he said as his hand brushed over the mottled "space age" themed surface, complete with silver flakes and elliptical circles circa the 1960's.

"I know. It's the character of this house. When we re-do the kitchen, then I'd like some granite. But nothing wrong with this the way it is. I hate throwing out something that can still be used."

"Exactly. And we'll remove everything carefully so Coop can sell it at the flea market." He laughed. Then he remembered that day before he left on deployment, the day that had changed everything.

The purchase of the house had taken up most of the money her father had given her from her mother's estate, so they were being frugal. They knew it would be a few months before another deployment came up, so they did what they could and planned everything else out in stages.

"Come, let me show you," Tucker said as he picked up several brushed chrome light fixtures and two long boxes of towel racks, entering the master bathroom. She followed him.

He held up the light bar that would be installed over the sink.

"I saw some mirrored medicine cabinets that would work great and will fit here. I'd like you to see them first," he said.

"Sure. I like the way that looks. I totally approve. The racks go nice with all that too."

"I got one that matches for the guest bath. I think I found a plumber at the store who said he could install a shower over the tub there. We're kind of stuck with this thing," he said as he pointed to the tiny tiled shower.

Brandy came up behind him and hugged him. "Mr. Hudson, this will be the nicest tiled closet anyone has ever seen. It's the perfect size. All we need is tension shelves."

Tucker gave his approval.

They liked to eat dinner upstairs in the "observatory," as it was now labeled. Brandy found the narrow stairwell comforting and knew it would be even nicer once she was further along. Tonight, she ordered some Italian food and had a nice bottle of red wine breathing on the folding table that was their fine dining area for Tucker. She had a bottle of cranberry mineral water for her.

It was getting to be near time when the food would be delivered. She took out a clean tablecloth, some silverware and two wine goblets from her boxes downstairs and set the table with some roses she'd found growing wild in the miniscule back yard. Tucker followed her up.

"I'm starved. When does it arrive?"

She checked her smartwatch. "About twenty minutes."

"Let's get this wine poured. Is it ready?" he asked.

"Whenever you want."

She stood in front of the large picture window that faced the Pacific Ocean. The sun had begun to hang, but it was still an hour until sunset.

"My queen," he said as he handed her the goblet with her fizzy cranberry juice. He toasted them and, before he drank, gave her a long kiss. "Who knew, Brandy, we could live this way?"

"You've come a long way, baby." She giggled. "Remember that dumpy apartment with the Big Booby magazines on the coffee table. Those things were awful!"

Tucker took a sip of his wine. "Guilty as charged. That was before I had the real thing."

His kiss this time lingered down her neck, headed toward her cleavage.

The doorbell rang. It sounded like an apartment buzzer.

Tucker stopped and grimaced. "That's the next thing I'm going to fix. We need a decent doorbell. I'll be right back."

Brandy watched from above as Tucker paid the driver. He pointed to two wooden crates containing young palm trees that had been placed at the side by the front stoop.

The driver shook his head, waved and returned to his car with the plastic "Flo's Pizza" sign attached to the roof.

"Hey, Brandy," Tucker called out while he was climbing the stairs. "Where did you get those palm tree?"

"I never saw them before. They must have just arrived."

Tucker set the food on the table, but they both went over to the window and examined the boxes, and then looked at each other.

"Not another package," Brandy said.

"Fuck."

In a flash, he was drilling down the stairwell. Brandy carefully followed behind him at a much slower pace.

An envelope was affixed with a piece of stretchy gold twine. On the outside was written,

To Brandy and Tucker, from a grateful friend.

Tucker let the note drop back against the palm tree base.

"Well, open it. You can't be serious to think it's a night letter, now, do you Tucker?"

"I don't want to touch it."

"Well then, I will."

She reached for the envelope and Tucker stopped her, holding her wrist tight and then putting his body between her and the trees.

"Tucker. What's going on?"

"I think I know who it's from. No, it's not a night letter. But it's not something I want to accept."

"Tucker, it's one of those fancy palm trees. You know how much they cost? Like one hundred dollars a foot. And there's two of them! No, wait, they're the cluster type, so we got, what Five? Six palm trees in each box?"

"I'll get something to wheel them out to the street,

and someone else can enjoy them."

"Tucker, you're being an idiot." Brandy struggled to remove her arm from his grip.

"I'm protecting my tribe."

Something odd had come over her husband. A dark mood lingered from something she knew was being kept as a secret.

"Look, I'm sorry." Tucker gently slipped his arm around her waist. "Let's eat first, and then we can have a chat. I'll open the envelope up after that, okay?"

She was moved by the softness in his voice and agreed.

They ate silently, watching the roses and peaches of the sky above the ocean, until at last the sun set and a bright green light formed at the last minute before it fell below the horizon and out of view.

"We got the flash!" he said.

His face was bathed in an orange glow as he continued to watch the sunset.

He was the phenomenon in the room, she thought. He was the handsome warrior who had brought life and love to her world, who had turned a life of frustration into a fairytale.

Green toads and danger along the way, of course.

She smiled at her own internal thoughts.

"What's got you laughing?" he asked.

"You. I'm so grateful I met you, Tucker. I can't imagine what my life would have been like without you."

"Nah, someone else would have swept you off your feet." He leaned across the table and gave her a kiss. "You're so easy to love, sweetheart. I think I'm the lucky one."

"When I think of what I was trying to be, it was like stuffing my personality into the mold of what I thought a girl should want and have and dream for, just like that bustier at Dorie's wedding. You remember that contraption?"

"Who could forget? To see you trussed up like that, it was such a turn-on."

She frowned.

"Don't be that way. I'm all mixed up, I admit. I love all the ampleness of your body. I always have. You're perfect for me."

She sipped the last of her mineral water and then set the glass down. "Okay. So now we're having that chat?"

Tucker looked up at the ceiling, rolled his head, and sighed. He leaned forward, put his arms on the table, and fiddled with the roses, causing a couple of petals to drop.

"At the hospital, Colin Riley came to visit."

"Who is he?"

"He's the benefactor, the one who helped out with the trip. He arranged the special flights, rented the big house on Gran Canaria, arranged the cars, everything. We couldn't have done it without his support."

"Okay. And?" She knew there was more to the story.

"We rescued his daughter. You know that."

"I do. You guys did a great job."

"Yeah, well, it spilled over, of course. You got dragged in, and—"

"And I shot them."

Tucker winced. "Yes, Brandy, you shot them. Thank you very much for that."

The cat-and-mouse conversations they had were so much fun for her. She loved seeing him spill something he didn't want to tell. It was impossible for him to tell her a lie or to hide his fear, although he tried.

"What about the hospital again?" she said, angling her head.

"He came to thank me. And he did."

"End of story? Somehow, I don't think so."

"He gave me his card and said sometime he'd like to talk to me, share ideas, and that stuff."

"And?"

"Well, you know, Brandy, I can't share what I do with anyone. I'm not supposed to have those conversations. I could lose my clearance, be out of a job, and I love my job."

"He offered you a job. I knew it."

"No, he didn't. He wanted to talk."

"So talk to him. He's a billionaire."

Brandy had suspected something had happened that night at the hospital, because Tucker had been hell-bent on renting a car and driving her home. He'd practically fought the nurses on staff to get her released. He made quite a scene. She knew something had caused that. And Brawley wasn't talking.

"I want to see the envelope. If it's what you say, there shouldn't be anything you can't show me. Or is there?"

"No, Brandy. I have no secrets."

"But you do."

"No, I don't." He wrinkled his brow. "What are you talking about?"

Brandy stood up and walked to a bag of groceries and plucked out the Big Butt magazine she'd pulled from his gun bag when they moved. It was frayed and dog-eared. But it was one of his, and she knew he'd been saving it as one of his favorites.

"Geez, Brandy. I didn't know I still owned that."

She loved the look on his face as she slowly placed the magazine in front of him. "Consider it dessert," she whispered in his ear.

She headed for the stairs and then stopped.

"Are you going to join me on the front porch?"

Tucker leapt to his feet and slipped past her, running down the stairs ahead of her. She met him on the outside. He removed the envelope, opened it, and took out a cream card. Brandy looked over his shoulder at the distinctive handwriting.

Brandy and Tucker,

As I've said before I can't thank you enough for your wonderful gift of my daughter's life. These trees should reach the height of thirty feet or more, so I hope you will plant them where you can enjoy watching them grow, as you grow your family and enjoy your new home. But don't place them anywhere they will spoil that fantastic view.

I'm glad our paths have crossed. I hope someday to be able to be more a part of your lives. During the time these trees grow, and hopefully before they get to be thirty feet, and I'm gone, I'd like to sit down and thank you in person and talk about a future that could be for all of us.

Thank you again,
Your friend,
Colin Riley.

Tucker's eyes were filled with tears.

"Honey?"

"Well, I was just thinking. Can you imagine how he

feels, losing a son and nearly losing a daughter? And let me say just this, knowing he gets to spend the rest of his life with her is payment enough. He doesn't need to thank me. I've lived with death before, and it's terrible. I've had people die in my arms. I thought we lost Brawley at one point. I thought I lost you."

She hugged her big man with the big heart.

"No, Tucker, you'll never lose me. Not ever."

Did you enjoy SEAL's Rescue? Stay tuned for another new book coming out later in the summer, featuring this wonderful couple, SEALed Protection, Book #5 of the Bone Frog Brotherhood.

Do you love to binge read? If you are new to my books, a great way to get acquainted with the SEAL Brotherhood world is to get the

Ultimate SEAL Collection #1

This contains books 1-4 of the original SEAL Brotherhood Series, plus two bonus novellas.

But you know you want more? Right? Why not purchase the next in the series,

Ultimate SEAL Collection #2

This 3-book set starts with a cross-Atlantic cruise with SEALs and their wives, and ends up with a ship hijacking, including an international cast of hundreds, and three thousand guests.

Here's how you can stalk me:

Website: sharonhamiltonauthor.com

Newsletter:

sharonhamiltonauthor.com/contact/#mailing%20list

Facebook: facebook.com/SharonHamiltonAuthor

Twitter: twitter.com/sharonlhamilton

Pinterest: pinterest.com/AuthorSharonH

Amazon:

amazon.com/Sharon-Hamilton/e/B004FQQMAC

BookBub:

bookbub.com/authors/sharon-hamilton

Youtube:

youtube.com/channel/UCDInkxXFpXp_4Vnq08ZxMBQ

Soundcloud:

soundcloud.com/sharon-hamilton-1

ABOUT THE AUTHOR

NYT and USA/Today Bestselling Author Sharon Hamilton's SEAL Brotherhood series have earned her author rankings of #1 in Romantic Suspense, Military Romance and Contemporary Romance. Her other *Brotherhood* stand-alone series are: Bad Boys of SEAL Team 3, Band of Bachelors, True Blue SEALs, Nashville SEALs, Bone Frog Brotherhood, Sunset SEALs, Bone Frog Bachelor Series and SEAL Brotherhood Legacy Series. She is a contributing author to the very popular Shadow SEALs multi-author series.

Her SEALs and former SEALs have invested in two wineries, a lavender farm and a brewery in Sonoma County, which have become part of the new stories. They also have expanded to include Veteran-benefit projects on the Florida Gulf Coast, as well as projects in Africa and the Maldives. One of the SEAL wives has even launched her own women's fiction series. But old characters, as well as children of these SEAL heroes keep returning to all the newer books.

Sharon also writes sexy paranormals in two series: Golden Vampires of Tuscany and The Guardians.

A lifelong organic vegetable and flower gardener,

Sharon and her husband lived for fifty years in the Wine Country of Northern California, where many of her stories take place. Recently, they have moved to the beautiful Gulf Coast of Florida, with stories of shipwrecks, the white sugar-sand beaches of Sunset, Treasure Island and Indian Rocks Beaches.

She loves hearing from fans through her website: authorsharonhamilton.com

Find out more about Sharon, her upcoming releases, appearances and news when you sign up for Sharon's newsletter.

Facebook:
facebook.com/SharonHamiltonAuthor

Twitter:
twitter.com/sharonlhamilton

Pinterest:
pinterest.com/AuthorSharonH

Amazon:
amazon.com/Sharon-Hamilton/e/B004FQQMAC

BookBub:
bookbub.com/authors/sharon-hamilton

Youtube:
youtube.com/channel/UCDInkxXFpXp_4Vnq08ZxMBQ

Soundcloud:
soundcloud.com/sharon-hamilton-1

Sharon Hamilton's Rockin' Romance Readers:
facebook.com/groups/sealteamromance

Sharon Hamilton's Goodreads Group:
goodreads.com/group/show/199125-sharon-hamilton-readers-group

Visit Sharon's Online Store:
sharon-hamilton-author.myshopify.com

Join Sharon's Review Teams:

eBook Reviews:
sharonhamiltonassistant@gmail.com

Audio Reviews:
sharonhamiltonassistant@gmail.com

Life is one fool thing after another.
Love is two fool things after each other.

REVIEWS

PRAISE FOR THE
GOLDEN VAMPIRES OF TUSCANY SERIES

"Well to say the least I was thoroughly surprise. I have read many Vampire books, from Ann Rice to Kym Grosso and few other Authors, so yes I do like Vampires, not the super scary ones from the old days, but the new ones are far more interesting far more human then one can remember. I found Honeymoon Bite a totally engrossing book, I was not able to put it down, page after page I found delight, love, understanding, well that is until the bad bad Vamp started being really bad. But seeing someone love another person so much that they would do anything to protect them, well that had me going, then well there was more and for a while I thought it was the end of a beautiful love story that spanned not only time but, spanned Italy and California. Won't divulge how it ended, but I did shed a few tears after screaming but Sharon Hamilton did not let me down, she took me on amazing trip that I loved, look forward to reading another Vampire book of hers."

"An excellent paranormal romance that was exciting, romantic, entertaining and very satisfying to read. It had me anticipating what would happen next many times over, so much so I could not put it down and even finished it up in a day. The vampires in this book were different from your average vampire, but I enjoy different variations and changes to the same old stuff. It made for a more unpredictable read and more adventurous to explore! Vampire lovers, any paranormal readers and even those who love the romance genre will enjoy Honeymoon Bite."

"This is the first non-Seal book of this author's I have read and I loved it. There is a cast-like hierarchy in this vampire community with humans at the very bottom and Golden vampires at the top. Lionel is a dark vampire who are servants of the Goldens. Phoebe is a Golden who has not decided if she will remain human or accept the turning to become a vampire. Either way she and Lionel can never be together since it is forbidden.

I enjoyed this story and I am looking forward to the next installment."

"A hauntingly romantic read. Old love lost and new love found. Family, heart, intrigue and vampires. Grabbed my attention and couldn't put down. Would definitely recommend."

PRAISE FOR THE
SEAL BROTHERHOOD SERIES

"Fans of Navy SEAL romance, I found a new author to feed your addiction. Finely written and loaded delicious with moments, Sharon Hamilton's storytelling satisfies like a thick bar of chocolate." —Marliss Melton, bestselling author of the *Team Twelve* Navy SEALs series

"Sharon Hamilton does an EXCELLENT job of fitting all the characters into a brotherhood of SEALS that may not be real but sure makes you feel that you have entered the circle and security of their world. The stories intertwine with each book before...and each book after and THAT is what makes Sharon Hamilton's SEAL Brotherhood Series so very interesting. You won't want to put down ANY of her books and they will keep you reading into the night when you should be sleeping. Start with this book...and you will not want to stop until you've read the whole series and then...you will be waiting for Sharon to write the next one." (5 Star Review)

"Kyle and Christy explode all over the pages in this first book, *[Accidental SEAL]*, in a whole new series of SEALs. If the twist and turns don't get your heart jumping, then maybe the suspense will. This is a must read for those that are looking for love and adventure with a little sloppy love thrown in for good measure." (5 Star Review)

PRAISE FOR THE
BAD BOYS OF SEAL TEAM 3 SERIES

"I love reading this series! Once you start these books, you can hardly put them down. The mix of romance and suspense keeps you turning the pages one right after another! Can't wait until the next book!" (5 Star Review)

"I love all of Sharon's Seal books, but *[SEAL's Code]* may just be her best to date. Danny and Luci's journey is filled with a wonderful insight into the Native American life. It is a love story that will fill you with warmth and contentment. You will enjoy Danny's journey to become a SEAL and his reasons for it. Good job Sharon!" (5 Star Review)

PRAISE FOR THE
BAND OF BACHELORS SERIES

"*[Lucas]* was the first book in the Band of Bachelors series and it was a phenomenal start. I loved how we got to see the other SEALs we all love and we got a look at Lucas and Marcy. They had an instant attraction, and their love was very intense. This book had it all, suspense, steamy romance, humor, everything you want in a riveting, outstanding read. I can't wait to read the next book in this series." (5 Star Review)

"Dear FATHER IN HEAVEN,

If I may respectfully say so sometimes you are a strange God. Though you love all mankind,

It seems you have special predilections too.

You seem to love those men who can stand up alone who face impossible odds, Who challenge every bully and every tyrant ~

Those men who know the heat and loneliness of Calvary. Possibly you cherish men of this stamp because you recognize the mark of your only son in them.

Since this unique group of men known as the SEALs know Calvary and suffering, teach them now the mystery of the resurrection ~ that they are indestructible, that they will live forever because of their deep faith in you.

And when they do come to heaven, may I respectfully warn you, Dear Father, they also know how to celebrate. So please be ready for them when they insert under your pearly gates.

Bless them, their devoted Families and their Country on this glorious occasion.

We ask this through the merits of your Son, Christ Jesus the Lord, Amen."

By Reverend E.J. McMalhon S.J. LCDR, CHC, USN
Awards Ceremony SEAL Team One
1975 At NAB, Coronado

Made in United States
Orlando, FL
26 April 2023

32506633R00104